Tomboy

TOMBOY

NINA BOURAOUI

Translated by
Marjorie Attignol Salvodon and
Jehanne-Marie Gavarini

University of Nebraska Press
Lincoln and London

Garçon manqué © Éditions Stock, 2000

English-language translation © 2007
by Marjorie Attignol Salvodon and
Jehanne-Marie Gavarini. All rights
reserved. Manufactured in the United
States of America ∞

Publication of this book was assisted
by a grant from the
National Endowment for the Arts.

NATIONAL
ENDOWMENT
FOR THE ARTS

A Great Nation Deserves Great Art

Library of Congress Cataloging-in-Publication Data
Bouraoui, Nina.
[Garçon manqué. English]
Tomboy / Nina Bouraoui ; translated
by Marjorie Attignol Salvodon
and Jehanne-Marie Gavarini.
p. cm. — (European women writers)
ISBN 978-0-8032-1363-0 (cloth : alk. paper) —
ISBN 978-0-8032-6259-1 (pbk. : alk. paper)
I. Salvodon, Marjorie, 1967–
II. Gavarini, Jehanne-Marie. III. Title.
PQ2662.07755G3713 2007
843'.914 — dc22   2006100949

Designed and set in Quadraat by A. Shahan.

Acknowledgments

I thank the people who helped make *Tomboy* possible: Jehanne-Marie Gavarini for her friendship, patience, and dedication; Véronique Vaquette, Jean-Philippe Salvodon, and Mark Schafer for encouraging me from the very beginning with steadfast support and love; Laura Pirott-Quintero, Shay Youngblood, Nancy Goldstein, and Michael Reder for reading good drafts and not so good drafts; Florence Hertz and Irline François for being great friends and allies in our search for the *mot juste*; the staff and faculty of the Department of Humanities and Modern Languages at Suffolk University, especially Barbara Abrams, Sandra Barriales-Bouche, and Celeste Kostopulos-Cooperman for comic relief, chocolate, and writing inspiration; and Luce Attignol, Jean-Léon Salvodon, Man Cia, and Mè Ta for unknowingly honing my interpreting and translating skills in all of our languages when I was a child. *Mèsi anpil.*

Marjorie Attignol Salvodon

I want to thank Marjorie Attignol Salvodon for trusting the project from the beginning and for being such a positive force on this earth. Thanks to my family: Laurence Gavarini for leading the way; Clifford Lehman for teaching me so much about the English language and for still being there for me after all these years; and Brigitte Parot and Ann Creely for their love, intellectual stimulation, and unconditional support throughout the years. I am also thankful to Mark Schafer for his help with sticky passages and to Véronique

Vaquette for introducing me to Marjorie and for her intelligent insights. Thank you to Dean Carroll, Provost Wooding, and Associate Provost Esterberg at the University of Massachusetts–Lowell, who supported and understood the importance of this book by awarding me a course release.

Jehanne-Marie Gavarini

We thank Nina Bouraoui for the strength of her words. They moved and sustained us through the lengthy process of translation. We warmly thank Ladette Randolph from the University of Nebraska Press for giving Tomboy an American home. We are grateful to our reviewers, especially Laura Rice for her careful reading, which made all the difference in the world.

Tomboy

ALGIERS

I'm running on Chenoua Beach, running with my friend Amine. I follow the foam-filled waves, white explosions. I'm running with the sea that rises and falls beneath the Roman ruins, running in the still-warm winter light. I fall on the sand. I hear the sea advancing, the sound of freighters leaving Africa. I belong to the sand, the sea, and the wind. I am in Algeria. France is far away, behind the huge and dangerous waves. It is invisible and imagined. Amine and I fall together. I hold his hand. We are alone, and we are foreigners. His mother is waiting in the white car. She is cold. She stays inside, protected from the waves, the wind, and the nostalgia of the Roman ruins. She is waiting for our race to end. Amine could be my brother.

Men emerge from the dunes, four of them. They are in a hurry. They walk hastily toward the sea: a meeting. They sketch grand gestures with their arms. They are speaking Arabic. Their voices carry across the beach, echoing in the waves and the wind. I feel mesmerized. They brush against our bodies and continue walking past us, their arms reaching toward the horizon. I remember one word only: *el bahr, el bahr, el bahr.*[1] Repeated enchantments.

Do they know about France? Are they awaiting the next freighter? Do they know that the sea is infinite?

They leave the beach without looking at us. We don't exist. I start the race again and laugh. I'm happier than Amine. The sea sustains me. It engulfs everything and obsesses me. The sea comes before the dream of France, before the journey. It was there before I felt fear.

1. The sea, the sea, the sea.

Amine's eyes are sad. Here, we are nothing. Born of French mothers. Born of Algerian fathers. Our bodies alone reunite the conflicting lands.

≈≈

My Algerian life is full of anxiety. I run, dive, and cross the street quickly. The street is off-limits. Rue d'Isly, rue Didouche-Mourad, rue Dienot, Le Telemny. The street on the other side of the car window is forbidden, unreal, and filled with children. The street is a dream. My Algerian heart beats outside of the city. It belongs to the sea and the desert at the foot of the Atlas Mountains. Here, my body is erased and becomes unrecognizable. I become a nondescript body, a body without language, without nationality. This life is brutal. It is voiceless and faceless. Agitated, I sleep badly and eat little. Amine mirrors my insanity. We run together, faster and faster. We flee.

We devour one another.

I leave Algiers far behind and head toward the silence. I return transformed, sensitive. I stay in my room. I talk to myself for a long time. I have a secret. I come from an uncommon union. I am both France and Algeria.

I'm protected from the street, the voices, the gestures, the stares. I'm fragile, they say. They exclude me. Amine stays with me. Always. He keeps the secret. He is the secret: it's in his skin, his eyes, and his accent. We change our names. We pretend to be in France. The RTA[2] shapes our dreams. It broadcasts powerful images that haunt us for a long time. It's as if another world has trespassed the borders of our own confined world. I know the dialogues, faces, and music. I learn fast, mimic, and memorize everything. We never stop playing this game. We build a wall, a prison within a prison.

We overthrow the city.

≈≈

2. Radio-télévision algérienne.

Amine's father returns from Tizi-Ouzou with two white burnouses. Gifts, he says. We put them on right away, pulling the hoods down over our heads. We cross our arms inside the wide, unsown sleeves. We disappear. Walking across the garden, we take small steps.

The burnouses are too long. They cover our whole bodies, drowning them. We become fragile and lost in the traditional dress that betrays our inability to live out a part of ourselves. We will always hesitate. We will never be real Algerians. Despite our will and longing. Despite the clothing. Despite the land that surrounds us.

Amine can say a few words in Arabic. His accent is too perfect. I don't respond. I am no longer playing. I distance myself. I know our limitations. I'm aware that proficiency is followed by feelings of incompetence. I know the difference that separates us from others, the difference in our blood.

I know vertigo, Amine.

Who are we?

His mother takes a photo of us. She will send the image of her son in disguise to her family, her French family. She'll spread our lie. The dog is circling us. He is barking at the two imposters.

≋

I don't speak Arabic. My voice says the letters of the alphabet, â, bâ, tâ, thâ, then vanishes. It's a ravenous voice, a voice that is a stranger to the language that it enunciates. I say words without understanding them.

Despite our hopes, it's a language that does not stick. I take courses in classical Arabic. They are required. They call us the Arabists. I learn the grammar and forget it. It's a fleeting language that escapes me, a slippage. I pronounce the very difficult hâ and rhâ. I recognize the sounds of el chekl.[3] But the meaning escapes me, leaving me empty.

I study Arabic for fifteen years, submerging myself deeply into my silence. I hold back, not understanding the voices that rise from

3. A group of signs that indicates the pronunciation of each word.

the streets. I invent another language, speaking Arabic in my own fashion. I interpret and keep lying, out of habit.

This language slipping through my fingers like sand makes me suffer. It leaves its scars, a few words, and disappears. It doesn't take to me. This language rejects me. It separates me from others and disrupts my lineage. It's an absence. I am powerless, an invalid and a foreigner. My land slips away from me. I am here, different, and French. But I'm Algerian: it's in my face, my eyes, my skin, my body inhabited by the body of my grandparents. I bear within me the smell of their house, the taste of pancakes and croquettes, the color of dresses, the songs, and the noise of jangling bangles. I remember Rabiâ's hand on my feverish face. I remember Bachir's voice beckoning his children. His voice rises above everything else. It continues to resonate, satisfying the longing. His voice is eternal, powerful. His voice links me to others, uniting me with the land, connecting me to Algeria.

≈≈≈

My mother makes me a foreigner by her mere presence at my side: her blond hair, her blue eyes, and her white skin. She walks down the street, squeezing my hand, holding my body close to hers. She draws me to her hip. It's our last stroll. My mother is a challenge. She is aware of it. She walks by the men without looking. Her eyes reach all the way to the sea. She spurns the city, a dark, dense forest outlined against the luminous sky. She's in danger. I am here. I protect her, despite myself. My unrelenting gaze bristles. The men brush against us and keep walking. They whisper. A child is a perfect excuse, a protection. A child cuts like a blade. I become my mother. I become her dress, her scent that lingers behind, and her coveted skin. A hand touches her hair then retreats by the sheer force of my merciless face. To touch. To know. To understand. My mother is a treasure. Amine and I take the place of our fathers. Finally, we are two real Algerians.

≈≈≈

A French woman says to my mother: "Why is there so much furniture in your house? Some day they'll take everything. Why put on makeup? They don't see us. Why put on perfume? Nothing takes here. Scents turn sour. The heat burns through the skin, to the flesh. For now we are stationed in Algiers. Then we'll do West Africa." On Moretti Beach a young man is drowning, way out there, lost already, so far away. He calls out. She speaks again: "Why go out there to save him and risk one's life? There are so many of them. All these brown bodies, packed together, all these people."

Ignoring this disapproving voice, my father runs toward the sea. He swims swiftly, pulled by the other voice, the voice of the drowning man. He is already there, lifting the body. He swims back to shore, burdened. He lays a young Algerian down on the sand. It could be his brother Amar. It could be the body of Amar, who was killed in the war. It could be his older brother missing in action, his lost love. He massages the young man's chest for a long time, doing mouth-to-mouth resuscitation. He waits for a sign, for life, as the silent swimmers form a circle around the two bodies, blocking the light. Nothing separates them. My father doesn't belong to me. He belongs to the other people who look on, overcome with sorrow. They feel all alone. The sea is a kind of violence; its waves, its sound, and its smell are constant.

The drowned man is thin and brown-haired. His face is smooth. His eyes are half-closed, as if he were dreaming. His belly is still, like a dark stone glistening with water. His hair is plastered down, his lips still wet. This man is dead. I'll never forget him. Every man I meet will bear this image, a ghostly face that destroys childhood. He could be you, Amine. Your face. Your lowered eyes. Your hair. His body could be yours, on the edge of adulthood. He'd follow you like a shadow or a twin. But you're not really Algerian. You only look Algerian, stricken by this French blood that gnaws away at you.

≈

Only Amine knows my games, my mimicry. Only Amine knows my secret desires, my childhood monsters. I take on another name:

Ahmed. I throw away my dresses. I cut my hair. I make myself disappear and assimilate into the world of men. I am shameless. I endure their gaze, steal their ways, learn fast, and change my voice.

I'm not afraid of the men of Zeralda. They take over the entire beach. They dive in the water all at once, without wetting their necks, stomachs, or ankles first. They are tough. They take over the sea with their cries, their movements, their numerous bodies. They are violent. They are alive.

I adjust my blue terry cloth bathing suit. I walk with a boyish gait. I am intrigued.

Amine likes me as a boy.

We stay on the beach until the edge of night. The last hours are pink, timeless, and slow as the fire of the sun becomes a mere memory on the sand, the skin, and the hidden pine forest. We are still playing. Defying the swift approach of night, I play fast. I am methodical. I hold onto the ball as long as possible, with my head, torso, and bare feet: my fearless body. I run, in tune with the sound of the sea. The waves are voices. The freighters' siren beckons to the men of Zeralda. They come. The siren draws in all these restless bodies.

I sense the tenderness of the men of Zeralda, their interest, their indulgence. They applaud. I learn how to be in their presence. I learn how to show myself, transformed. They look at me. My body itself captivates them. My lie becomes public: by my rapid gestures, my aggressive attitude, and my broken voice. I become their son.

Here, I am the only girl who plays soccer. Here, I am the child who lies. My entire life will consist of repairing this lie.

Revisiting it. Erasing it. Being forgiven. Being a woman, becoming one finally.

My entire life will be shaped by the loss of the gentle gaze of the men of Zeralda, although they misperceive me.

≈≈

The game continues at the school in Petit Hydra. It's a challenge. It's an obliteration. I displace my female self. I am always chosen by the boys' team. I play against my team. I play my role. My strength is not in my fragile body. It is in my desire to be other, passing in the world of men. I play against my female self.

I play despite my small size, my fine skin. I play in the rain storms. I'm not afraid of the sky's might flooding the gardens and Hydra Plaza. The gaze of the men of Zeralda gives me courage, allows transgression—in spite of other people's words, small scars forever etched in my flesh.

My clothes. My appearance. My running. My endurance is a kind of madness. My voice. My soaked hair. My bloody legs. My flight. My discarded identity.

The indulgent gaze of the men of Zeralda stops the rumblings.

I watch the boys in the street after school, playing with the newfound sun. It sparkles. How they mirror my rage. I can't get out of the car. They fall and knock each other over. They dribble the ball between the trolley cars, playing with death. They're not afraid of anything. My hand on the window begs to play. My gaze will always be full of envy. They are my age. They have my skin. They have my hair.

I don't understand all their words. "Yahya Algeria"[4] is constantly repeated. I repeat it in front of the mirror in the long hallway that separates the bedrooms. I hear the crowd's voice, singular, like an invocation. *Yahya Algeria.* I'm as one with those children.

I play inside my prison. I become Dahleb, the soccer player who signs his photograph, "To little Nina, with all my affection." The affection of the men of Zeralda returns to me, and the tenderness of Amine's eyes that look without saying a word. Silence is agreement.

So, I become his double. I leave his shadow, taking his strength. I will always protect Amine. The earth that bears us is my witness.

≈

I go to the French school. I go to the French high school. I go to the Alliance française. I go to the French Cultural Center. France is still here in Algeria, projected, diminished, and marginal.

4. Long live Algeria!

I speak French. I hear Arabic. My summer vacations are French. I am on Algerian land. I run on Algerian sand. I hear my Algerian father's voice. I am with the multiracial children. Being together, we understand each other.

I am not very familiar with Algerian families; still, I turn down French families' invitations. The way they look at me. Their words. Their judgments. Their French Algeria. Arabic words infiltrate my native language, incursions. I end my sentences with *hachma*.[5]

I have two passports. Yet I have only one visible face.

Algerians don't see me. French people don't understand. I build walls that separate me from other people. Others. Their lips and their eyes search my body for a trace of my mother, a sign of my father. "She has Maryvonne's smile." "She has Rachid's gestures." Forever split between this one and that one, enduring a fractured identity, seeing myself as divided. Who do I look like the most? Who has conquered me? Who has won over my voice? My face? My body in motion? France or Algeria?

I will always have to explain and justify myself. These eyes will follow me for a long time. They'll feed the fear of the other, this foreigner. Only writing will protect me from the world.

≈≈≈

Who will I be in France? Where will I go? How will the French see me? To be French means being without my father, without his strength, his eyes, his guiding hands. To be Algerian means being without my mother, without her face, her voice, her protective hands. Who am I? Amine will choose at eighteen. He will choose his camp. He will become whole. He will defend only one country.[6] He will finally know. As for me, I am both horribly free and restrained.

"You're not French." "You're not Algerian."

5. Shame.
6. As a male citizen of both countries, at eighteen Amine will have to choose whether he will do his military service in France or in Algeria.—*Translators*

I am everything. I am nothing. My skin. My eyes. My voice. My body closes in on itself twice over.

I stay with my mother. I stay with my father. I take from both. I lose from both. Each part merges with the other only to separate again. Each part kisses and quarrels. It's a war. It's a marriage. It's a rejection. It's a seduction. I don't choose. I leave and I return. My body is born of two exiles. I travel inside myself. I run, immobile. My nights are Algerian. My memory brings back the faces that shape my own. My days are French: elementary school, high school, the French language we speak. Amine speaks of France, the other country, the one that he longs for in its absence.

≈

Amine raises his voice over the sound of the waves that flood the Sidi-Ferruch dike. He tells stories of a land beyond the black stones of the Algerian reef. He talks about France and the other childhood, about his French life. He searches for words, calls out, but can no longer remember. Other voices contradict his: the voices of the sea, the wind, and the birds. He wrestles against the strength of the surrounding land. First it's a struggle, then a protest. He unearths his other face, my foreigner. We walk on the dike, against the violence of the sea and the wind that dictates its movements. We are between France and Algeria, captured by the Southern winter, a false season. Here, the sun is eternal. I no longer hear Amine or no longer want to hear him. His dream. His desire. He is already elsewhere, without me. His French life requires my absence.

My life finds its pulse here. It is made of the sea, the earth, and the domed houses of Sidi-Ferruch. I know Algeria, her cycles. France is a kind of violence. It will snatch me from Algiers. I am different from Amine. I know our places: Cherchell, Tipaza, Boufarik. Treasured places. I learn to assimilate, to be less conflicted. France is outside of me. I run away. I always return to Algeria. I know this place, its Roman ruins. My solitude is here, with these stones. France remains white and impossible. It witnessed my birth and my departure. A rejection. I am reborn in an apartment in Algiers, the Gulf,[7] September 1967. This is where I invent myself. It is here that I create my face, my eyes, my voice. Everything is done here, in the midst of my Algerian solitude. I will always be from here, shaped by the lessons I learned in the Algeria of the 1970s.

Our mothers are in the streets of Sidi-Ferruch, their hands protecting their faces from the wind. They bow with the gusts of salt and sand. The violence of the sea is all that exists, a battle. Fragile bodies against the sound of the waves. Amine is gone. They do not notice. Amine gets lost. They could care less about Amine's disavowal, his separation from Algeria, his desire, my madness.

Amine is attracted by the dark blue waves. Amine is split and pulled by that other country. Amine celebrates his victory over me. I am abandoned. I run toward my mother. She holds my shoulders. We struggle against the wind. My mother draws me to her waist. She heals everything. I close my eyes. Amine is here. Filled with despair, his body is in Algeria.

The wind ceases. The waves die down. Silence overtakes the place. It resembles death. We go back to Algiers. The car follows the edge of the rocks. The sea, its dunes, its reeds, and its reefs lead to the city. The sea disappears as the first villages appear. Koléa. Boufarik. Douéra. Flags. Alleys of plane trees. Inflatable mattresses, beach balls, and flotation devices.

A child is playing alone. Men are leaning against the city's walls. Boredom settles in. Women are hidden. Desire. This is Algeria, Amine, its fragility. The siren of the freighters reminds us of the sea, of its intoxicating smell. Amine is leaning against the car door. He is thinking about the elusive sea, a shadow in the night. He is voiceless. I know his sadness. I know his inscrutable face.

We will never be like everyone else.

≈≈≈

7. Neighborhood in Algiers.

I become Algerian through my father, his protective hand in my hand, his hair, his eyes, his brown skin, and his voice. I become Algerian through his Arabic tongue, his prayers, his parents inhabiting his body like occupiers. I get in his car with delight. I watch the street, his neck, the buses, his shoulders, the children, his hands always slow and supple. I accompany him to Hydra Plaza. We get out of the car. I hold onto his arm, a concrete anchor. I walk with my legs wide open. I am with my father. I believe I am becoming Algerian. I am saved.

My father initiates me into childhood. He raises me as a boy, his pride. Grace of a girl, agility of a boy. I have his will, he says. He teaches me how to play soccer, volleyball, how to swim the crawl, how to dive from the brown, shiny rocks, just like the hoodlums.

He gives me strength. He molds my body. He teaches me to defend myself in the country of men. To run. To jump. To run away. He wards off my fragility. He calls me Brio. I'm not sure why. I like this name; it draws out my silhouette and physical traits. Brio stretches out my muscles. Brio is the light on my face. Brio is my will to live. The men of Hydra Plaza. Their hands in my hair. Rachid's son or daughter? His eyes, his skin, his narrow shoulders. His girl. Their fingers pinch my cheeks, their smell reaches my nose. Here, I am protected by their words, their slow gestures, their attitudes, their faces. Later I will mimic them. Here, I notice and learn. Here, I share in the secret of the men of Algiers.

≋

I organize my life secretly. I become my true self in my room. It's the place where I can mimic to my heart's content. I conjure up reality, then modify it. I walk in circles. I am looking for someone else. I stand for a while in front of my open window looking onto the Mitidja plains. I count the electrical poles that mark the hillsides. I count the red balls delicately strung on the taut cables. The wind makes the cables vibrate. The runway lights shine at night as a warning to airplanes. This vibrato. These lights. This is Algeria at night. A night without silence. A frightening night.

The sea is literally on the other side of the apartment. It is blue in the winter and white in the summer. Black freighters go across it. The sea is violent. Its beaches are tucked away, invisible from here. The Bay of Algiers forms a ridge. It's a defense against the sea. It's a wall that wards off invasion. It is city life, packed, noisy, and organized. It's not my life.

Only the large chimney of the Telemli factory stands out from the terraces. It pierces the sky. The sea is behind the eucalyptus grove. I am always looking beyond. Beyond the Mitidja plains. Beyond the trees. Beyond my female body. Beyond the sea is France, my native and neglected homeland. The sea is cradled by two continents. I remain between these two countries. I am between two identities. My equilibrium lies in my solitude, a unifying force. I invent another world, without a voice, without judgment. I dance for hours. A trance followed by silence. I learn to write.

≋

The sand of Zeralda Beach is ashen, burnt by the sun. The sea retreats. It is bottomless. It becomes unfit for swimming. It heads for foreign shores, abandoning us. The beach is immense. Frequently deserted, it magnifies solitude. The solitude of swimmers, of Amine's mother, of my listless body. I only have the sea, the sand, the vista of distant reefs, the movement of clouds, the sky, my own vertigo. I only have nature, through which I become adult and learn about desire. I am attracted to her.

I came with Farid M. to this very place on a field trip. I held his hand for a long time. I refrained from swimming. In the heat, in the din of the surf, in the violence of the Algerian summer. I came to Zeralda Beach without Amine. I became a girl here, by Farid M.'s presence. I recognized my face in his eyes. I heard my voice in his slow, secretive voice.

Amine's mother, with her white skin and her face, confronts the sun. It's a war. She is powerless here, on the Algerian beach. She only hears the sea, her escape. She is crushed by Algeria. More than a foreigner, she's a French woman. She says nothing. She can't tolerate the sun. She covers her legs. The heat. A bite. She is looking for her place here in Zeralda, yet she remains on the outside. She's a child without a country.

The sun burns Zeralda, the sea, and my tanned body. The sun burns the white skin of the French woman. It falls on bodies, muffles voices. We can't hear each other. I return to Amine, my sad friend. He runs off and comes back. He is running away from his mother and from the earth. Algeria is his prison. I envy his body. I want his long muscles, his precociously adult face, his rough hands, his shoulders, and his curly black hair.

I am too small for my age.

The beach is impossible. It suffocates. It isolates. Amine's mother is not with us. She is not watching. She is obsessed with the sun. It targets her body, consuming everything. It announces the imminent danger of this country. The sun is violent. It burns the salt and kindles, heating up the stones on the cliffs. Its light is white. Its rays are powerful.

The sun is madness. The sun is a man who devours Algeria. We run away from the beach and the doomed body of Amine's mother. We leave the blaze. We are headed to Zeralda's hotel. We climb a wall. We cross the gardens with dirt under our bare feet, brambles poking our thighs, and reeds slashing our skin. The silence returns, spreading beyond the white archways. It enters the mosaic walls. It permeates the deserted hotel. It lurks beneath the blue water of the pool. It is present in our boredom.

The sun reaches Zeralda's hotel. I jump off the diving board. I go down, deep, and I stay at the bottom for a long time. The sun scorches like fire against my breath, against my will. It is waiting for me. I don't resurface. The sun uncovers the truth: I am not Algerian. The sun burns the row of pine trees. It is looking for me. It is coming. Its oblique rays consume me. The sun is a kind of vengeance. I am not from here. I will not resurface. I remain seated at the bottom of the pool. I am underneath Zeralda. I am underneath the earth to drown my boredom, the face of Amine's mother, the solitude of our abandoned bodies, and my Algerian life. The pool is deep. I hear my voice in my throat. I hear my own blood. To drown in Algeria. To conquer the sun and to stay here. Never to return to France. Amine descends into the pool. His eyes are open. I see his face, his beautiful face. Amine has his father's face. He grips my shoulders. He alone knows; he knows the force of the sun and my fragility. He lifts me up. His belly against mine. My head on his chest. Amine is no longer a child. Slowly, we resurface. We will remain haunted by the secret of the pool.

≈≈≈

I am a foreigner here; I am nothing. France forgets me while Algeria doesn't know who I am. Here, identity is molded. It is dual and broken. Here, I avoid the children's gaze. I don't understand the language.

Two bastards on the beach. Two mixed-race children. Amine and I. Me and Amine. Attracted to each other. Sitting side by side. Cuddled up in the water, forever. Difficult children, as the women say.

Here, I look for my land, and I search for my face. I remain outside of Algeria. I am inadmissible. Here, I hate France. Here, I know hatred. Here, I am the French woman's daughter. The child of the Roumia.[8] Here, I bear in me Algeria's War of Independence. I dream of being an Arab in honor of my Algerian grandmother, Rabiâ Bouraoui. In memory of her hand on my forehead, her belly, her blood, her language that I don't understand, her tenderness, and her son, Amar, who was killed during the war.

Here, I carry the wound of my Algerian family.

I keep Amar's photograph, my secret. It's his last photograph, shot on the battlefield. Dressed in military uniform, he is cocking a

8. *Roumia* derives from the term *Roumi*, which is used by Muslims to designate Christians.—*Translators*

gun and aiming at the photographer as a joke. He aims at the camera lens as a reminder of the pain, the battle, and French Algeria. He takes aim at the child who looks at the photograph. He wears a cartridge belt. He is a man at war. A white house stands behind him. It's his post. His routine: his sleep, his meals, and his watch. He smiles, aiming at my entire French family. Amar is the oldest son, who passed away. Amar is the lost brother. Amar is my father's silence, his separation. Amar appears at night through the last photograph of him, my obsession.

≋

My white mother replaces the freedom fighter. My father chooses a French wife soon after his brother dies fighting the French. I am in the midst of the Algerian War of Independence. I bear the conflict. I bear the absence of the eldest son of the family and the memory of his disappearance. His body is never found, remaining like a secret in the maquis. He lays in the dry dirt, at the top of the cliffs, under the sun that fans the fires. He remains in the midst of the Algerian blaze, under its red horizon and dark clouds. The mountain will never be the same. My father looks at Amar's photograph. He searches for him, though he also will need to forget this loss. Amar's death is unreal. It's a kidnapping, a disappearance. It's a bottomless image and an endless mourning.

My mother brings France back to Algeria by her mere presence, her will, her love for this independent country, and her French family. "You will not marry an Algerian." My mother loses all her ties except for my father, her children, and her new land. The land of Amar.

By her mere body, my mother reconciles; by her mere hands, she unites. But she is not successful. Her face. Her skin. Her hair. Her eyes. Her freedom. My mother in the streets of Algiers, at the beach, in the driver's seat, in the family home, under the fire of the Algerian freedom fighters. My mother cannot be but a French woman in Algeria.

≋

For a long time I believe I am an anomaly, the result of a wrongdoing. I am forged by the war. I come from a controversial marriage. I bear the suffering of my Algerian family. I remember the rejection of my French kin. I carry these transmissions. Violence no longer leaves me. It inhabits me. It comes from me. It comes from Algerian people who invade. It comes from French people who disown.

For a long time I keep Amar's photograph. I invent his story. For a long time I trick reality. I become Amar. I play at being a man. I am captivated. Violence precedes my birth. Violence will return to Algeria, breaking out between its inhabitants. I become violent. With myself. With others. I search for my identity. My gaze is often sad. I resemble my father struggling to remember Amar. His photograph. My new role. I cut off my hair. I throw away my dresses. I run fast and fall often. I always get back up. I don't want to be Algerian. I don't want to be French. It's my strength against other people. I am nondescript. It's a war against the world. I become unclassifiable. I'm not ethnic enough: "You are not an Arab like other Arabs." I am too ethnic: "You are not French." I'm not afraid of myself. My strength defies hatred. My silence is a battle. I will also write because of this. My writing will be in French, while my last name remains Arab. It will be a desertion. But which camp should I choose? Which part of me should I burn?

≈≈≈

Born of a French mother. Born of an Algerian father. I know the smells, the sounds, and the colors. It's an asset and a liability. Not choosing makes me a nomad. My Algerian face. My French voice. Both light and dark, an internal conflict. I am made up of two warring elements, two jealousies that devour each other. In Algiers's French high school, I am an Arabist. Some teachers place us on the right sides of their classrooms, opposite the real French children, the children of overseas volunteers. The Arabic teacher places us on the left side of his classroom, opposite the real Algerians. Arabic doesn't stick. There's slippage.

Writing will rekindle this separation. French writer? Maghrebian writer? Some will choose for me, against my will. This will be yet another violence.

The desert is actually in France. It is immense and permanent. It is in the city, the walls of Paris. I will not be able to exist over there, where Algeria is known only through immigration.

Who will understand about the children of the 1970s? Who will understand about the marriages that took place after Algerian independence? Who will understand about the insane desire to be loved? Two countries. Two solitudes. Who will read about this violence? Only nature gives us strength, reconciling and exerting its power over my body; it both overwhelms and shelters me. This is why nature is inhuman.

≋

The silence of the earth enchants me. This is how the secret is born. It will follow me for a long time, along with the lie.

My silence is an omission. Who will know what I am made of? The Algerian earth is a man as well as a woman who nourishes my body. It will give shape to the regret, to my fear of others, my fear of their destructive rumors.

Amine jumps from the slippery black rocks. His hands reach toward the abyss. His muscular body, brown skin, closed eyes, broad shoulders, and peaceful face: Amine. A prayer. We scale the cliffs of Rocher Plat for days, clutching the stone, fighting against vertigo, against danger. We are alive, connected to a life force and the madness of our childhood. Danger is within us; it's not in the cliffs, the deep sea, the sun, or the heights. Danger is rooted in us: it lurks beneath our skin and expresses itself on our faces. It shows in our abnegation, in our homesickness. It comes from separation. Born of French mothers. Born of Algerian fathers. Two orphans facing the void.

Here, the sea forms a tight and narrow channel. It is transparent on the surface and dark at the bottom. Amine says: "When you feel the water, slow down. Otherwise, you'll crash into the rocks." To crash, to hit, to hurt oneself: it's a death-defying jump. It's a challenge aimed at the other boys who are jumping, who are jostling me, and who take my turn. Amine imposes me on them and protects me. I know how to dive. They are jumping in the water two at a time. Backwards. Sideways. They are all wearing black swimsuits. They are still screaming: "Yahya Algeria!"

A woman climbs the cliff. She is neither Algerian nor French. She's a good swimmer, they say. She doesn't dive; she offers her body, her impulsion, her suppleness, her strong shoulders. "Paola," her son calls out. Her first name is Paola. Her husband is looking for her. She goes back up fast, clinging to the wall like an animal. She waits her turn standing close to me. She says: "You are handsome." I don't respond. I dive and hide my face. I dive, full of shame. I don't resurface. I hate the sea. I hate the divers. I hate France. I hate Algeria. You are handsome. I remain with this violence, staying put under the sun that reveals my disguise. You are handsome. Amine corrects her, protecting me. This is Nina. She's a girl. Amine defends himself: he wouldn't like a boy that way. He likes the girl I am, this fake girl. It's his madness for this ape, this transvestite. Paola says: "You are even more beautiful if you are a girl." I don't answer. I don't know. I don't know myself.

Paola: her legs, her lips holding a cigarette, her insistent voice. Paola: her belly, her skin. She stays on the rocks and looks at me as if adopting me. Her voice and her dives. Her gnarled woman's hands. Her cigarette smoke on my face, its smell mingling with the smell of salt. My shame is an infinite silence. My shame seals my life.

The sea engulfs everything. I look at it with all my strength. The sea retreats. I hold it back with my mere body that is still partially facing Paola's body. I remain balanced. I remain off balance. Paola. I pray at night. I pray to the sky. I pray to Amine.

Paola. For a long time I will hear her voice.

≋

My life is a secret. I am the only one who knows my desire. Here in Algeria I want to be a man, and I know why. It's my only certainty. It's my truth. To be a man in Algeria means becoming invisible. I will leave my body, my face, my voice. I will be on the side of power. Algeria is a man; it is a forest of men. Here, men are dark shadows packed like sardines. Here, men are alone by dint of being together. Here, men are violent from their unfulfilled desire. This desire is a loss that cannot be traded. It's extreme, going from hot to cold. It comes from boredom. It comes from fantasy. This desire is unappeased and permanent.

To be a man in Algeria is to lose one's fear. Here, I am terrified: their eyes, their hands, their bodies against the high school gates. I never look directly at them; I just feel them. They wait. My eyes, my body, my voice: objects of consumption. Here, men are sad. They lean against the walls, facing the sea and smoking. They are still waiting. The sea is a desire; it is miraculous. The sea is a lie. They dream, like Amine. They hope, but they no longer sing.

They invent departures and imagine arrivals. They will do better than others and experience the French dream. Their gaze is a weapon, their hands burning embers, their desire a conflict. They hurt themselves, alone. They are fragile. I like them because of it. They don't know that.

As for me, I know France, I know disdain, I know endless war, Amine. In France you will be a foreigner.

In France you will not be French.

In France you will not be mixed-race. Your skin is white, but your hair is too black. In France you will not be a good Arab. You will be nothing: born of a French mother, born of an Algerian father. In France real Arabs will not like you. You speak with an accent; you speak with your hands. You need to touch your friends. But you don't speak Arabic. You have no knowledge of Algeria. You will have no knowledge of France, Amine. You will remain outside of your homeland. You will look at the sea from the other side, and you will lie. Algeria will no longer remember you.

In France you'll hear: "dirty Arab," "sand nigger," "rat." You will defend yourself. And they will say: "But we're not talking about you." It will cause pain. You'll be willing to be a sand nigger. But you are nothing, Amine. You will have a strange face, strange skin, bizarre eyes, such a rare color. In France you will be neither French nor Algerian. You will be nothing, and you will be everything. You will not even be a man uprooted from Algiers's forest of men.

≈≈≈

Isolating myself from my body, I could lose myself in the streets of Algiers and let the bodies of men invade me. I will become a body that waits. Here, time is infinite and exhilarating. It is a prison. Time goes against men, unbeknownst to them. Each day is a kind of violence; each instant is an explosion. Since 1970, Algerian violence has been in the streets. It comes from time's immobility. It is in these foraging bodies that walk in circles and proliferate. Each person is someone else's mirror as well as his defeat. Each sadness gets passed on; each body gets contaminated by another. Everyone shares a common heritage, forming a single body in the end. It's a unique movement, an attraction. Algerian time is an illness; it impoverishes and misleads. It is inside bodies, creating a protective coating. It hems in. It is disillusion itself. I don't know the streets. I see without crossing: Paradou Street, Gulf Street, Zirout-Youcef Boulevard. I no longer know the Casbah. I no longer go there. I don't know Bab el-Oued. It's off-limits. I know nothing about downtown Algiers. I know everything about the desert: the one tree in the Ténéré, the Tassili plateau, the trenches of the Hoggar. I know how to walk with the stars. I don't know how to walk with men: how to become a man in Algeria, enter the game, follow the concentric circles. I am caught in the spokes, trapped in the bowels of the city.

With men, I will become a man, a body without a name, a voice without a face. I will assimilate and become an element, a fragment, one of the shadows among them. My existence is too much. I am a woman. I remain outside the forest of men.

I know my house, La Résidence, the park, the seven buildings that together form a circle, L'Orangeraie. I don't know the streets, from which I am banned. I don't have the right to go out alone since the event. The street is my enemy. The street is a real body. It is men's turf: my exclusion. The street is dense, a nonplace. It's a concentration, a heap of flesh. Murmurs. Whistles. It's a faction. It's the street that makes me crazy. The street is the exact opposite of the desert. Here, men arm themselves against two contradictions: the sea and the desert. Here, men arm themselves against two of the biggest vertigos of Algeria: the advancing desert and the engulfing sea with its waves, its freighters, its passengers who go from the port of Algiers to Marseilles on the Djazaïr boat. People go up and down the gangways, always carrying heavy loads. Coming and going. They always return to Algeria. They go from the sea to the street, from vertigo to the absence of vertigo. A fall.

The desert is without men. Since the event, it's my refuge. I have access to the desert, not to the street. The street is a pit full of men.

The street is full of bodies, and these bodies walk with the rats, out of habit. Here, rats are bigger than cats. Here, rats devour cats. Here, rats attack dogs. When rats start eating dogs, men on the street will become the target of the rats. Here, rats look for small children: that's why we live on upper floors. That's why we close the windows at night. We suffer the heat. Our fear of the night is in fact a fear of rats. Rats enter apartments because they are attracted to the smell of milk. They disembowel infants and inhabit their cradles.

I run the risk of becoming a rat that creeps along the forbidden streets.

Since the event, the street is off-limits. The brown man lurks there. The street shelters him. I don't know anything about him, not even his name, but I know that his face is as sharp as a knife. I know his well-trimmed beard, a ring around his red lips. His eyes are black, his skin very white, his hair very dark, and his body lanky. He is young, wears a suit, and is handsome. He leans toward me to speak, bending just like a reed. He speaks close to my face. All I hear is his voice, his offer. He speaks in French. He's Algerian. He comes from Algiers. He is calm and his gestures are slow. He has all the time in the world. A presence in his white shirt and black suit, he smiles often, knowing how to seduce me. He says: "You are beautiful." I am still a girl in his eyes. He says: "Come with me." I'm not afraid. He smells good. I could follow him, fall in the fire and burn myself. His nails are filed, and they shine in the sunlight. He wears a wristwatch and a leather belt. He says he has been watching me for a long time. He's waiting. He's waiting for me near the orange trees of La Résidence. He knows my games, my solitude. He knows my childhood innocence. Is it the scent of fruit or the smell of his skin that swirls around me, encircling me? Is it his voice or the silence of the park that drowns me?

He's wearing shoes with laces. He takes my hand, repeating constantly: "You are beautiful." It's a whisper. "What's your name?" It's a prayer. All of Algeria contains this man. My entire childhood veers toward him. He touches my hair and says it's silky. He caresses my face and says it's like velvet. His hands, his gentleness, his beard, and his eyebrows. He holds the whole world in his hands. He says: "Come." He looks around. I am not coming. I stay put, next to the orange trees, under the blue sky; my body is my only defense, my wound. It's nothing, and yet it's everything. It's the rape of my face, my eyes, and my skin. It's the violation of my trust. It's an immense betrayal. It's a stranger who holds the nape of my neck. He has already destroyed my childhood, unknowingly. He takes it away. Is it the cry of the sea or my sister's scream that reaches us? Is it a wind gust or my sister's strength? Is it the rain that pummels or the speed of our gait? Is it an escape or another game? I don't know. I no longer know. I don't want to know.

For a long time I will hate the screams of children at play, resenting their tears, their fragility, their milky skin.

It is trivial, and yet it is monumental: his hands touching my face, his words brushing against my eyes, his voice reaching for my closed lips. His attention, his desire, and his gentleness are an immense brutality: his Algerian violence.

Amine, didn't you know that a man tried to kidnap me? Didn't you know about all the children who disappear in Algeria, about my sister's intelligence, her speed? Didn't you know, Amine, that she saved me with her child's strength? Long after the event, we will play in the orange grove, and I will tell you that it is my favorite place.

≈≈≈

It's nothing. His offer, his attempt; yet it's already everything. His voice still echoes. This man is in my life. He makes the decision, and childhood comes to an end. This man is my defeat. Never will I give my hand. Never will I yield my face. It's nothing, and it's already everything. This man is at the root of my fear. This man embodies fear: my fear of noise, the street, and screams. The memory of his features will linger. He will return by day and at night. This man is the death of other men, their hands and their voices like armed shadows behind my back. For a long time, my head bent, I walk along the walls of big cities, my body hunched over. I shun men. My rage strikes their faces, my hatred confronts their desire, and my gestures counter their gentleness. For a long time I will carry this injustice. I don't want to hear. I shut men out. A case of blindness and renunciation. Was it more than his palms on my cheeks? Was it more than his wrist on my arm that felt like shackles? Was it more than his breath on my skin? His tenderness, a robbery. This man has stolen my mother's hands. This man takes me for his child, and more. He claims the girl. I will become a man to avenge my fragile body.

Who else knew? Who else saw?

What else is there but the smell of the orange grove, this blue sky, and my sadness? The blue Algerian sky makes me cry: its purity, its bottomless beauty, its grandeur so tranquil, its indifference. The blue Algerian sky takes over and presses down, a cold ember that spreads. The blue Algerian sky makes me suffer. It exacerbates poverty, the solitude of my imperfect female body, the solitude of men who wait against the walls under the wisteria, between the orange trees.

This man sets the street on fire. The street becomes dangerous and male. Was it more than our escape, a struggle, a few slaps, and a tear? Did I feel his belly, his thighs, or his shoulders against my body? Did I feel his lips kiss mine? My sister confronts the culprit. She trades her body for mine: a sacrifice.

I don't remember. But I know. This man makes me lie. It was only an attempted kidnapping.

Is it he who just rang the bell? Is that his face behind the peephole? My sister climbs on a chair to look and identify him. My sister leans against the door, a partition. Our separation. His body returns, haunted by my face. My sister takes a knife to defend me and becomes my mother. It is the man again, his breath behind the door. My vertigo.

Does he know where the lobby of my building is, what floor I live on? Does he look at the window of my bedroom from the street?

What kind of night did I spend afterward, Amine? I don't remember; it happened in a flash. My memory doesn't go back there. It's a forbidden place inhabited by dreams. It's a camp, a concentration. These are my wounded years, Amine.

I often disguise myself, betraying my female body in order to forget the man's voice, erase his soft hands on my face, and deny his intention. My childhood ploughs through the desert of this man who disappears until adulthood, at which point I recover my memory and recall the stranger. His features blend with my own, his mask covering mine. I become a travesty. I am alone, without my sister, without Amine. It's a negation. It's a game. I reveal the secret when I leave my bedroom. The silence of other people exposes the fallacy.

I plaster my hair back, carry a whistle around my neck, and place a fake gun in my back pocket. I square my shoulders, open my legs, and wear jeans for the first time. I am the only one here in Algeria to have jeans from Washington DC, thanks to my father's assignments abroad. His trips in exchange for my pants. I trade his presence in Algeria for perfumes, clothes, and foreign goods. I have all my father's trips to become a man. I have all his time, all his absences to replace him, and all his flights to transform myself. I have all his ocean crossings to marry my mother, to save and protect her.

His numerous postcards correspond to the number of ties I steal from his collection. Easter Island, Belgrade, Santiago in Chile, Vienna, and Moscow. I experience his every return as a confirmation of my victory. My father invents Brio and leaves Brio behind. You will watch over the house. His departures are the root of my desire to change, to transform myself. I become Brio. After his long trips, my father's voice returns as an unreal song whose tune I had forgotten. He will often say "first class."[9] To be the first in everything. To be a boy, shaped by the grace of his actual daughter. First class

9. "First class" is in English in the original French text.—*Translators*

for my sister as well. To be his beauties, his children to whom he returns. Not to understand his long trips but not to say anything. To be proud of his airline tickets, conference name tags, World Bank stationary, and foreign pencils: symbols to bring back, tokens to use. I feed on my father. Brio confronts the man of the orange grove. Brio stands up for all of Algeria. Brio stands up against all of France. Brio battles my own suffering body.

Brio stands up to the woman who says: "What a beautiful little girl. What's your name?" Ahmed. Her shock. My defiance. Her unease. My victory. I make the whole world ashamed. I soil childhood. It's a wicked game, child's play. She's a perverse child. Brio stands up to the shoe salesman. "Sandals? Ballerina slippers? Buckles?" No, I want my father's shoes. Those shoes, the black ones with laces. The shoes of the man who tried to kidnap me, the one who thinks about me at night. No, I don't want to get married. No, I won't let my hair grow long. No, I won't walk like a girl. No, I'm not French. I become an Algerian man. *Yahya Algeria.* Yes, I still want my father's shoes, those that cross America and that always separate us: Redford's, McQueen's, and Hoffman's shoes. The shoes from the RTA's images. Travel shoes. The shoes of absence. Men's shoes. For a long time afterward I will erase the separation with my own trips to Boston, Cape Cod, and Provincetown, following in my father's footsteps. Much later I will finally feel at home, far from Algiers, far from Rennes, under the immense trees of New Hampshire.

By dint of playing, I win. I know the man's smell; my new scent is an illusion. Drops of Fabergé on my shirt collar. I know the man's desire. I know his madness. It makes me dizzy. My body is at the center of the earth. I shatter my identity. I change my life. To feel my firm stomach, my muscular chest, my strong shoulders; to deny myself. To see another face in the mirror. To talk to oneself. To think of oneself as virile: it's a sin. I punish myself with the wind that sweeps through the atrium of La Résidence, the hail that bends the trees in the eucalyptus forest, and the violence of Algerian thunderstorms. I castigate myself with the torrents of mud, the resuscitated wadis,

the swelling, darkening sea, and the humidity. I pay with the cold
that falls on the Roman ruins, the soaked paths of Mount Chréa,
the cold wind of the Chiffa canyons, and the wet bodies of mon-
keys living in cliffs. I get sick. Often. I withdraw to my room, to my
bed, defying the stares of other people. Something is not right with
Nina. She's not normal. We must let a doctor see her, cure her. She
will have problems later. No, not at all; she is feminine. She puts
cream on every night. Loads of Nivea cream. It's once again a mis-
understanding, a stolen gesture. Nivea is my shaving cream.

I conceal my body. I learn to suffocate, hide myself, and no longer eat. My eyes devour my face.

Nina, with her Indian eyes.

≈≈≈

I often come to your house, Amine. You live in a low house with
an enclosed garden. It's not like the park of La Résidence, which
is large and dangerous. It's not the eucalyptus forest, the sound of
the wind in its trees. From here you don't see the sea or the city of
Algiers. It's a hidden house. A safe place. I'm afraid of your dog
Zak, a German shepard. He rushes toward me, always. He smells
my fear. He grabs my shoulders with his paws, scratches my back,
and licks the nape of my neck. He really kisses me, and I don't like
it. His belly is firm and smooth. You rescue me from Zak by kicking
him, but he starts up again. He's stronger than you, Amine. His is
a dog's strength. You say that he's in love with me. You're so naïve.
Often I compare men with Zak. His violence is like a magnet on
my skin. It's a leech that sucks my blood. The hell your dog raises
comes from my odor. My body attracts him. We no longer play in the
garden because of Zak. I no longer play in the park of La Résidence
because of the brown man. We stay in your room, which is bigger
than mine. You are an only child, so I become your sister. We listen
to the same song on your record player. All I have is a red plastic
portable record player, a gift from my French grandmother.

It works every other time we use it. My grandmother says that the trip broke it. The plane. The distance. This country. This Algeria, her poison. This land takes her daughter and then her two grandchildren, Jami and Nina, whom she really loves. Of course. Rachid's daughters. So dark. And Nina, the more Algerian-looking one. The spitting image of her father: it's in her gestures, her small hands, and her gaze, which is troubling at times. Amine, did you know that I was born in Rennes, at the Hôtel-Dieu, and not in Algiers? She sends me records by airmail. It's Kader, the doorman at La Résidence, who brings them to me. Sometimes we listen to them together, but I think he doesn't like them. My records. My choices. Bad taste, says my sister. "J'avais oublié que les roses étaient roses," "J'aime pas les rhododendrons," and the song by Marie Myriam. It's my French side, my very French side. Then I listen to Dalida. "J'attendrai le jour et la nuit, j'attendrai toujours ton retour." Yes, mommy, I waited a long time during my French vacations. I waited for you to take me away from this sadness, from your absence during the entire month of August. I even waited for you in La Bourboule's little hotel room with my red plastic portable record player and Dalida's song. I waited to tell you about the vacation of the two foreigners in France.

You came back in the summer, looking stunningly beautiful, and you dried my tears tenderly.

We always listen to the same song on your record player, Amine. When our fathers are far from Algiers, on the other side of the sea. Their trips. Our solitude. Your father is often in Japan because of the salt factory. Here, we have salt lakes and salt flowers that we pick in the middle of the desert. You will do a presentation. You will bring salt crystals to class. It will be more than salt. You will hold your father's entire face in your hand: his eyes, his smile, his black hair. You will get a good grade. You know your subject tearfully. You know that your father is Algerian. You know his profession and your love for him. Our song "Ava Inouva."[10]

10. "Little Father" by Idir.

We repeat the Kabyle words without understanding. It's a language that already sings without music. It's a language for children. "Ava Inouva," our lullaby. We dance as best we can, with our laughter and our sadness. Still, excluded from this foreign land, we find it impossible and closed to us. We don't know the Kabyle language; we mimic it. Like the Arabic language, it's our invention and our misfortune. Tokyo–Washington DC. I will get a new pair of jeans. You will get a kimono. A Japanese kimono traded for the burnouses from Tizi-Ouzou. But you will never be Japanese, Amine. Despite your crossed arms and your small steps. Eventually, you will speak Kabyle, with just the right accent and with the correct intonation. But you will speak without the understanding, without the flesh of the language. You will speak a skeletal language only.

You are not Kabyle, Amine, despite your desperately white skin.

≋

In France you'll be mistaken for a Kabyle, Amine.[11] You will carry Idir's song like a tattoo. You will carry my voice that rises like a cry. They will decide for you, against your truth. You will be betrayed, but you will say nothing. Your silence is a sadness, a refusal, and an omission. In France it will be better to be Kabyle, better than being Algerian, and less complicated than being Franco-Algerian. You will look sharper, Amine, and you will quickly get used to this idea. It's a safety net. You will be a mysterious man, the man with angel hair and small hands. You will become a king. They will think they know your secret, your fire, your blood, your sad look, and your eyes that are so black. Kabyle is an upright man. It's a man who walks tall. Kabyle is your pride, a man with a raised fist and a tight belly. Kabyle is your strong shoulders and your muscular legs. You will like this new identity: your comfort, your secret, and your lie. You will get used to it and introduce yourself in this way. It will

11. Because of their light skin, Kabyle people are sometimes mistaken for white in France, erasing their actual ethnic origin.—*Translators*

always return like an illness. You are a Kabyle, that's for sure. You are not like the others. You will be free and freed from your parents and their story. You will no longer have to explain: I am the son of a French mother and an Algerian father. Kabyle puts the world at your feet, Amine.

Kabyle will bring together your two origins and shape your identity. To be unique, born of a single stem, a sole tension, a single lineage, a single family. North over South. White over black. You will leave childhood. You will leave me. You will leave us by way of your new people, your invention. You will remember Idir's song, the joy of this language. You will conjure up the songs, the costumes, and the colors of Algeria; you will become exotic, Amine. You will add local color to their French parties, at the university, and in their bedrooms. You will speak about these glances, these women, their worn faces, their resistance. You will speak about the Djurdjura Mountains, Amine. You will say that your sadness emanates from there. It's your Kabyle nostalgia and your depression. You will lie, Amine. You will erase your mother. You will erase your life in Algiers, your father's absences, and your Algerian fear. You will become a Kabyle in France. And you will be accepted. It will be like reexperiencing violence and separation. Without me there you will be scorched by racism, prejudice of skin color, and intolerance. And you will go even further; Kabyle will no longer be enough.

You will say: "I don't know a thing about immigration, deportation, or misery. I don't know a thing about factories, construction sites, or buildings. I know nothing about Harkis,[12] workers, their wives, or family reunification. It's not my story. It's not my misfortune. No, I am not a son of immigrants. No, I was not born in France. I come from the sea, the mountains, and the desert. Yes, I have white skin. My grandfather had blond hair, but I lost his photograph." And you will go even further, Amine: "No, I am neither

12. Harki is the term used to designate the North African military backup troops who served with the French.—*Translators*

like these foreigners with their suffering, nor like these second-generation children. I don't share their memories. I am really different. No, I don't know a thing about the other side of the tracks, these buildings beyond the ghetto, this concentration, these stairwells, floors, housing projects, and gangs." And you will go even further: "They scare me. I don't know how they live. I don't hear their voices. I avoid them. I go to the other side of the street and close my eyes. They know nothing about the Djurdjura. No, I am not like them. You see, I lost my accent. I no longer speak with my hands. I become French. I'm a calm man." You will be nothing, Amine. Your body in the streets of Paris, your dying voice, your solitude, your desert, your lowered eyes, and your hands inside your coat sleeves. The rain wets your hair and your spiritless body. Your abnegation turns you into a sad man. The Algerian who defends himself is like a drowning Algerian, the drowned man on Moretti Beach who should not have been rescued. Your so beautiful face is pinned to the ground. You will know. "Ava Inouva." They will dance to this song. They will ask you how to do it. Open hands, bulging chest, a swing of the hips — you will show them how a man dances around a woman, circling her. This will be your defiance, your revenge on your French victims. Your youyous,[13] your whistling, your clapping palms. You will remember. Remember the Algerian children who used to throw stones at us on our way home from the school in Petit Hydra.

You will remember, and you will carry our shame.

≈≈≈

"Ava Inouva." I frequently run away from my house and stay in Amine's room. I separate myself from La Résidence, like a lone body. Like peeling scorched skin, I tear myself away from this apartment. This seismic place is the scene of many crimes. I go from Yasmina to Nina. From Nina to Ahmed. From Ahmed to Brio. It's an assas-

13. *Youyou* is a vocal expression of celebration. —*Translators*

sination, an infanticide, and a suicide. I don't know who I am. One and multiple. Lying and truthful. Strong and weak. Girl and boy. My body will betray me one day. It will develop into a female body and turn against me. It will resist. I will hold on to Nina forcefully like a wild animal. We find champagne glasses wrapped in newspaper from 1962. We find bloody knives in the apartment. Blood from 1962. My sister is born at the time of the crime: the year of the massacre of the Algerian women from La Résidence, the year of the OAS[14] massacre. It was their last massacre. Their revenge. The curse is everywhere. In my room, all over the apartment walls, on the tile floor, and in the laundry room. We find their weapons and alcohol under the bathroom plumbing. This madness is the way the men of the OAS celebrated.

They tell stories from Building A to Building G, a rumor in La Résidence's semicircular buildings. This haunted place marked by its noises, shadows, and apparitions. The wind blows constantly: it's the complaint of the Algerian women massacred by the OAS men.

We must bathe in their blood. Be consumed by this fever. We must live with the image of these women with their slit throats, their cries, and the act itself. We ourselves cry at night about the massacre. Taking in the violence against my better judgment, I become violent myself. "Ava Inouva." Your house is different, Amine. It becomes my refuge. "Ava Inouva." You never dance with me or take my hand. My skin is on fire. My voice is dangerous. You don't touch me. You reject me. You still believe in childhood, in its innocence. I am impossible: impossible to leave, impossible to hate. So endearing. You look at me for a long time. You desire me in secret. Your mother wants to separate us. She compulsively repeats her obsession: "I don't want my son to become a homosexual." She says the word first. She says my word. Under this girl's influence, this fake girl, it might happen to him too. She is Amine's madness, his mir-

---

14. OAS (Organisation Armée Secrète) is the French right wing organization that engaged in terrorist activities to crush the Algerian independence movement.
—Translators

ror. They will be separated into different classrooms to stop them from being close. But it's too late; I've already taken from your flesh. I love you like a man, Amine.

For you, I invent myself with other eyes and other gestures. For you, I have the hands of a man, strong and clenched in fists. This is how I experience our Algerian history, in combat. Avenge Amar's death. Avenge my father and my mother. Avenge the Algerian women massacred at the hands of the OAS men. My fists speak to the urgency of this moment, this sacred time. They speak to the loss of the land that surrounds and shapes us, this land that catches on fire with its burnt Atlas Mountains like flushed cheeks. Our lives are raging flames, and I am dancing all around you. I am lighting up your body. "Ava Inouva." In France you will imitate me, copying my sexual dance, my way of approaching someone: to provoke, to ask, to seek. You never approach me. You wait for my signal, submissively. I penetrate you and I dance like a man. I teach you to walk like Steve McQueen. I teach you to play and swim the crawl without suffocating, going with the flow. One, two. Swimming in two strokes. In and out. Your life in two strokes. You, me, you, me. I am inside you, Amine. You are invaded.

You have long, black, curly hair. You cry for nothing. You whine. We call you the crybaby. You have temper tantrums. I intoxicate you. Your skin is so white, so fine. You lay dormant under a girl's skin. I teach you how to be strong. I love you like a man. I love you as if you were a girl. You give shape to the lie of my life. The whole world will get me wrong.

I should be rescued from you, Amine. I'm the one in danger. I am the one who needs to be treated, cured, and taken into account. I should not let this deviancy take hold. No one prevents me from being who I am. There is no prohibition from my family, my love. Nina is capricious. That's all. It's not serious: her clothes, her low-pitched tone, and the ensuing silence needed to soothe her cracked voice. Nina is an artist, so nervous yet so sensitive. She lives in another world, all locked up. We can't do anything about that. Nina is locked up from inside. I am the one who needs to be rescued and forced to speak. Speak, Ahmed! Speak, Brio! Only language rescues me. Where are you, Yasmina? Underneath, a woman suffocates, drowned and pushed aside. It should be told for those who follow. Prepare. Anticipate. My silence builds my future. I am never in the right place; I always remain on the outside. I never correspond to the projected image. The eyes of other people reveal my false beauty. To be beautiful before writing, that's the hell other people impose on me. That's what they will inflict on me.

I am the one your mother should save. Save me from her looks, her anger, and her perpetually accusing voice. Amine's excitability, his tantrums, his madness: He gets it from her. Nina is Amine's illness. Brio is Ahmed's brother. Nina is Yasmina's mutilation. Look at your daughter, Maryvonne. Look, why don't you. Open your eyes. See her ways on the street, hear the comments from waiters and salesgirls. When her cousins are dressed in white, she wears red and green. These are the words of my French grandmother. Her gaze says: "You're a tomboy." No. My audience is proud of me. I exist.

≈≈

The OAS men return every time my father leaves. Three women alone in the apartment, three memories, three fragile bodies. I am not strong enough. Everything changes abruptly with my father's trips, his suitcase, and his raincoat. It always rains outside of Algiers, on the other side of the sea. The smell of his *eau de toilette*. The elevator's door, the noise of the cables that pull it up and down. Then nothing, an erasure. Only details about the trip, the separation. His attaché case, his serious look, his sad look. He moves fast. He won't stay. No tears allowed. His folded suits, his row of shirts, his ties, and his shoes. Such meticulous preparations. Not to forget anything. To be elegant. The door closes. My sister locks it behind him, our forced retreat. From now on we have to protect ourselves from everything. My father is no longer here. Carried by the forceful jet engines, he is now beyond the sound barrier. He is abroad. He becomes a foreigner, a man alone. We don't know when he will return. Maybe never. It always takes a long time: all those oceans to cross, those meetings, and those conferences. The OPEP. The Group of 24. The International Monetary Fund. It's a hard blow. I am invisible. My body does not offset all these voices, translations, and world affairs. He doesn't divulge his return date, and so his trips become secrets. That's his foreign life. That's my desert.

But he always returns. Sometimes a month later, sometimes he stays longer. I don't know anymore. His absence is like dead air, a time to fill up. It's my time to transform. I await his postcards and his telephone calls, his worried voice. They never last long. The lines are bad. Algeria is congested. Other voices and children's laughter join our conversation. My father is this man whom I must share with his country, his work, my mother, and my sister. My father is the object of so many people's jealousies. He returns to spoil us, higgledy-piggledy. He brings back everything: a cowboy outfit, Caprice des dieux cheese, pasta shells, Kool menthol cigarettes, a Repetto tutu, and Cadum soap amassed atop the dining room table. It compensates for his absence. Material life. He comes back to love us, always more. It's Riyad the driver who watches us. He goes shopping: cream cheese, Nouna chocolate, meat, and vegetables. He takes his role as our substitute father very seriously. He protects us against the OAS men and the ghosts that haunt La Résidence. They visit my mother's body: through her chronic asthma, her long sleep, her solitude, and her fear. Yes, we're afraid. The ghosts return with the wind, the dark forest that separates us from the sea, the immense park, and the nightly roar of the power plant.

My mother is suffocating here, in Algeria: hands on her chest, inhalator, cortisone, and oxygen tent. Riyad the driver replaces my father. His professionalism, his way of being a man, his tense body, his very upright head, his hands on the steering wheel, his silence, his slamming on the brakes, his shaved nape, and his slightly protruding ears. The black Renault takes us to elementary school, high school, the sea, and the hospital. We go to the beach in the middle of winter. He lets me run like a madwoman on the wet sand, near the immense waves, where the walls collapse. I run alone with my strength and the monster that I feed. My father's cologne remains on the driver's seat. Riyad is waiting for me without saying a word. He bends his head, sometimes to the right, sometimes to the left, at odds. But he is lenient with me. He lets me race, my hair full of sand, while the wind stings my face. Riyad lets it all happen. It's his intelligence. Afterward I will sleep well, thanks to him. He brings me back home. I am his little sacred package. He closes the door. He has a duplicate key. Everything is okay. Everything is going badly. I'm afraid. I sleep between my mother and my sister. I sleep with my mother's breath, her asthma. My memory of the apartment: knives underneath the bathroom plumbing. Her visions. The blood will return, she says.

She's afraid for me because of her haunting dream. It's a stormy night. I am stretched out on railroad tracks, tied down. The train is fast approaching. We hear neither the scraping of the wheels on the rails nor its siren. The train is a silent and metallic mass. My mother can't do anything for me. She will not stop the train. She will not stop life, its slow and certain progression. I am crushed. Crushed by Algeria. Crushed by France. Crushed by my sensibility. Crushed by all my first names. Crushed by fear. It's Riyad who closes the door to her hospital room.

I still go to your house, Amine. We will say this to my father afterward, so as not to scare him. Your mother says: "I'll take Nina." Yes, she takes me, despite the risk. I don't want my son to become a homosexual. My sister is going elsewhere. I don't know where. Maybe to her friend's house. Girls stay with girls. Boys stay with boys. That's the way it goes.

That day your mother prepares grated carrots with a hint of lemon. I hate it. The grated carrots spoil my mother's body lying in the hospital. Spoiled is our winter vacation. Spoiled are the blue Algerian sky and my father's return. I wet my pants by accident. You lend me your favorite pants, Amine, a very tough thick, blue fabric.

I keep them for a long time. I take them hostage. I refuse to return them. Your mother protests. I live in your clothes, precisely where you hold your hidden sex.

Isn't it at this very moment, by this gesture, by this theft, that homosexuality takes hold?

My father's trips before Christmas are great. He brings back freedom, wind on his raincoat, perfume on his hands, smells of the plane, the airport, and his tough Delsey leather bags. He brings back sugar. Sugar with the cowboy hat, sugar with the motorcyclist outfit, sugar with New Man shirts. Sugar. It's what's missing here. It's Algeria's downside. Smarties, Carambar, and Chocoletti swapped for the salt of the sea. Sweetness on the tongue swapped for the arid Aurès Mountains, the drought of the old maquis, the burning cliffs that wind along the road to the Roman ruins of Tipaza. Swapped for the immortal dunes of the Sahel. Swapped for the sand and the void it creates in the city, drowning it. The sand is like the sea. It advances in waves and spreads quickly. It suffocates and destroys. It's a tidal wave, an insubordinate giant, the massive shadow of cities, and night falling like a threat. It's the fear of men. Someday the Sahel will overtake everything.

No trips, no gifts. So, before Christmas, we go on the prowl. My mother walks all over the city, despite being stared at, despite the dangers. She hunts like a she-wolf, a mother for her litter, for Remus and Romulus. We invent. We make roses out of tissue paper, cotton snowmen, and Christmas trees out of green felt. Christmas in Algeria is the North against the South. It's the snow against the sun. It's an unreal and often uncomfortable celebration.

We look in the pharmacy on Didouche Street. We pick records: Joan Baez, the song about Che Guevara, Reggiani, and Brassens. Our life is political; it's an adult life. We manage for Christmas, shopping as best we can, but it takes a long time searching through all these toys made in communist China. Imports. These little toys made by tiny Chinese hands, miniature objects for a big celebration.

I choose an unassembled skeleton, a Chinese skeleton. Amine, you'll get an electric train, new clothes, and men's cologne. You bring back all of that to our house. Your abundance. You act surprised as you open your gifts, but you already know. Your gifts. Your victory. You plug your electrical track in my bedroom socket. Your smell on my skin. Your jacket on the back of my chair. Your tissue paper on the floor of my house. Your invasion. You are being so French now. But I am fully Algerian. I am jealous, but I don't say anything. I will never be a little Chinese girl. My hands are too big. I have to fit the ribs in the spine, place the jaw under the ears, and put the hips and the pelvis together. Then it's time to assemble the thighbone, the kneecap, the vertebrae, and the back of the skull. It's not easy. It takes time to put a skeleton together — more time than your tracks, your cars, your gas station, and your bleachers. You're still playing with toys, Amine. But I am facing life with this skeleton. I am playing with death, this little skeleton. I am playing with you, Amine. I'm rebuilding you.

It's our last Christmas in Algeria. The celebration of the infidels.

≈

Enjoy this Christmas, Amine; it's the last one. Look carefully at the faces of my mother, my father, my sister. Remember their warmth and their unconditional love. Look at my face. Look at the Roman ruins of Tipaza, the trenches, the baths, and the walls hardly touched by the passage of time. Look for another room, another jewel, and another amphora one last time. Dive from the cliffs of Rocher Plat. Wear your body out plunging. Take advantage of the sea. It's our last swim. Look at the crashing waves and the sun that burns the horizon, Amine. Take in the dry desert air. Scream from the top of the Assekrem and wait for the echo of my voice. Run down the slopes, the dunes, and the vineyards. Remember these unknown faces. Remember our time together. Remember the villages of Boufarik, Cherchell, and Bérard. Cross the farms, the fields, and the Mitidja plains. Look at the Bay of Algiers to fix it in your memory.

Don't forget anything. Here, you construct your history; your present shapes your future. Now is your time for action. You are from here and remain from here: your voice, your gait, your gestures, and your silence. Remember the streets of the Casbah. Everything changes so fast. Everything falls. Everything rises against us. We are already at war, the recently declared war, the now declared war. Their stares on the beach. Our bodies noticeably naked. Their eyes behind the bushes. Their words. Their insults. Suddenly, everything quickens. Hatred returns. Hatred rises. They accuse us. They say: "You are second-generation *pieds-noirs*."[15] "You are colonizers." "You are still French." But we don't own anything. Our mere bodies, our faces alone, are invasions.

Look closely at my face, Amine, because you will miss it for a long time. My face is your face. My sadness is your sadness. You will want to remember, but you won't succeed. You will always miss something from Algeria, a piece of information or a detail. You won't be able to retain the whole story; it will slip away, fleeing as if seeking revenge. How did everything get toppled in Algeria? How did Christmas, the beach, the movies, the street become prohibited? How did nature become a prison? How did an entire people come to scorn us? No more smiles, no more warmth. Not one gesture, no longer anything. It will be necessary to protect ourselves and leave. Take my hand, Amine. It's almost the end of our story. We will leave behind the roses of Blida, the dunes of Algiers Beach, the farm of Rocher Plat, the small ladder placed against the most beautiful reefs in the world. You will search in the South of France, in Corsica, in Italy, in the Balearic Islands. But it will never be Algeria: a white country, an uprooted country, our country. Remember the paintings of the Tassili-n-Ajjer. Remember the Pouillon hotels in Timimoun, in Ghardaïa, in Tamanrasset. Remember the ochre colors that used to soil our swimsuits. This fire. This pigment. This fire of the earth,

15. Pieds-noirs is the term used to designate European settlers who lived in French-colonized Algeria.—*Translators*

this bloody land. Look again at my face, my eyes, and my lips. I, too, will change with this departure, with this abandonment of Algeria. Your wound will be my wound. You will leave yourself in Algeria. You will not find yourself in France, Amine. Keep your place here, still. Live in the moment. Reflect on your time. Everything will burn. Everything will be erased. Everything will disappear in Algeria: our voices, our steps, places our bodies now inhabit, our Algeria. You will not like the *pieds-noirs*—at least some of them. You will not like their ways, their words, and their regrets. They will tell you: "You're like us." But you will be different, Amine, so different. Unlike them, you loved the Algeria that belongs to Algerians.

You will feel alone, alone without me, alone and deported. You will look for me in Paris in other faces, in other voices, under the touch of other hands, and you will not find me. One by one, you will lose your new friends. You won't even fight it. You will let the ties come undone. This is your punishment. I will be in your mirror. I will be in your image. I will be in your head. I will exist, and you will not see me. You will be alone inside and outside of yourself. But who will truly know all this?

Amine, you don't know yet that you will miss Algeria like you miss someone you love: a man, a woman, or your own child. You think it's no big deal to live here. You think everything passes and is forgotten: this land, you, and me, the perfect triangle, your life in three movements. We are invaded, Amine. Your silence will come from my own. Our solitude will come from absence. Every fear will come from abandonment. This land shapes us. You will no longer be anything without it, without me, or without us. Amine, you don't know yet that its loss is unbearable, that it will bring terror. You don't know that imbalance will follow the massacres. They will kill each other someday, on the other side of the sea. Algeria will return like a ghost. Algeria will return through the small black door of an immense morgue. You will be haunted. Algeria will follow your shadow, consume your thoughts, wake you up at night, and lull your days. Algeria will cost you: your abandonment, your debt, your constant breakups, and your unsuccessful relationships. Death will slip in between you and other people. It will cost you. It will be your sadness and your violence. You will always be missing something, Amine. Your romantic breakups will be induced by the misfortune of this land. This is your curse, Amine: your stories, your agitated life, and your broken arm.

You will always travel the world holding Algeria in your hands. You will say your last name and your first name. You will introduce yourself in this way, despite your face, your white skin, and your strange eyes. It will be your challenge. You will scare people away sometimes. This imbalance, this excess, this slight strength measured against a great fragility, your inventions. They won't believe you, or they will find you violent, capable of doing anything. He's a backstabber, they'll say, a fake. Their meanness. You will carry their idea of Algeria: the Algeria of massacres, hatchets, blood, and hatred. In a dream you will go even further, betraying your memory, inventing your country, this new and unknown land. You will say: "I am Algerian." But you will know nothing of the Algeria of the 1990s, Amine. Your body, its gestures, and your laughter were elsewhere then. And you will always miss something from the years 1967 to 1981 in Algeria, this very thing that will prevent you from existing, from being happy, from giving, from sharing yourself and no longer being afraid. Who will you be, Amine? What will your Parisian life be like? They will think you are mad and lost. They will ask, but you will give nothing of yourself. Then they will become angry with you. They will not understand your silence, the voice you withhold, and the fists you clench. Our punches.

No one, then, will know your Algeria.

You will be incomplete, Amine. You will not be your whole self. You will always be missing something: a secret, a face, or a lost fragment. You will search like a madman, like a dog, like a lost son. Your memory will no longer suffice. Who will know your pain? You will want to write about it. The book of your life, a closed book, a poetic book, your incomplete book. You will not succeed in writing it. You will hide. You will remain a stranger to yourself far from Algeria. Eventually, you will find someone. It will not be me. But you will become intimate with her. You will get used to her voice, her hands covering your neck, the softness of her eyes. She will neither be your mother nor your father. You will meet her when you're a man. You will tell her about your fear, your longing, and your difference. It will hurt, but you will tell her about your two countries: France and Algeria. You will find your friend. Her name will be Anne F.

You will discover her silence and her contemplation. You will know her patience. Her eyes resemble mine. She listens to you for a long time and reads you like a book. You will find yourself in her Parisian life, but you will remain an Algerian. You will become more and more Arab, thanks to her. You will be her pride, her beauty. You will teach her about Algeria and tell her our story. This way, she'll know everything about you. She will know how to protect you, calm you, make you fall asleep, and wake you up. She will chase away your enemies, give you strength. She will conjure up Algeria through her voice and transmit your story to others, our past. Through you, she will become Algerian. She won't be me, but you will find me again, Amine. This will be your new world. This will be your solitude as well as hers.

≋

I no longer go down to the park of La Résidence. It belongs to the unknown man; it's his place now. It becomes the park of the man who attempted to kidnap me. I no longer go to Moretti. Algeria has become my greatest anxiety. I know the exact date when people's looks, gestures, and reactions changed. On the road to the Gulf neighborhood, my mother is driving when we are stopped by a group of children who built a barricade of braided lianas. They throw ropes across the hood of our blue Citroën and shower us with stones and spit. It's an ambush, as if all the children of Algeria had been waiting for us here, past the windy curves that border the woods. It's as if all the hatred from the war were coming back in a flash, with the power of the car brakes and the screeching tires.

We skid while the voices, the blows of the sticks against the road, and the punches of the Algerian children rain down on us. Childhood is the heart of the earth. These children are the death of this land. Some lower their pants; the body is more powerful than the voice. The body is more aggressive than words. Their tiny genitals. Their small weapons. They strike my mother. It's nothing, just the blows of children. They are mild, rough, awkward, and random. But it's an early symptom: this raised hand, this attack. It's an aggression of the child against the mother, of the Algerian man against the French woman.

≈≈

I no longer go to Zeralda Beach. The swimmers remain dressed in black pants and white shirts. Women wait in the cars, with veils on their faces and hands on their mouths. There is no one in the water. The sea is as beautiful as before, alone under the sky and deserted. Mother-Sea, bodiless. Men speak amongst themselves, watchful. Swimming is forbidden.

Zeralda is too close to the city, to its unease. One must go farther, toward Tipaza, Bérard, and Cherchell. And still, it's never far enough; it's always within Algeria's borders. We have to cover our skin and shoulders, hide our thighs and bellies. The sea has become a vice.

≈≈

We receive a package from an anonymous source: uncooked semolina. No note, no address, just a white package that is left at the door of our apartment. Neither a donation nor a gift, the semolina is wrapped in a rag that is still humid. We must throw it out. No cooking it or eating it. No! It's a curse. El Aïne. Uncooked semolina rolled with hands wishing us dead.

≈≈

The telephone rings in the middle of the night. No voice on the other end, simply the depth of silence, then a slow and loud breath.

A handkerchief on the handset, a muffled voice, some insults. It's often my mother who answers. She says "allô" in French.

≈≈

The four tires of our car disappear one morning. They have been replaced with stones, making it look like a prehistoric chariot, thus announcing the horrible immobility of this new era: the Stone Age.

≈≈

Someone throws a bucket of water on me as I leave the building. It comes from a balcony. A bucket of dirty water. The smell of urine on my clothes, a punishment for the daughter of the French woman.

≈≈

This will end in a bloodbath, my mother keeps saying.

≈≈

Some people talk about Morocco, others about Tunisia. We spend a few days in Spain, in Mallorca, needing to walk near the olive groves. Algeria is so much more beautiful.

≈≈

Your house is shut, Amine. The key is no longer behind the small rosebush. The shutters of your bedroom are closed because of so much sun. It burns the curtains and yellows the wallpaper. Zak keeps watch. When I walk by your house, he barks often at hidden shadows and at me. I don't stop. Your mother parks her car inside. They jimmied the locks. Who are they?

≈≈

I no longer go to Le Français cinema. A young man caressed my shoulder, then my arms as soon as the movie started. *The Good, the Bad and the Ugly*. I changed seats, but he followed me. I left the cinema full of hatred.

≈≈

The farmers hide behind the bushes of Rocher Plat. They look at bodies: the naked bodies of girls, my sister and her friends Selima, Fedia, and Manina. They watch them swimming and laughing. I watch them as well. We look at the skin of these young girls, their faces. They have a certain joie de vivre: their secrets, their cigarettes, palm oil, and salt crystals scintillate in their wet hair. It's an infinite violence.

≈≈

I no longer take tennis lessons with Mister B. because a crazy young man slashed the net with a sickle.

≈≈

There is a rat outside my apartment door. It's impossible to go in. The rat screeches, showing its teeth. I'm going to look for Kader, the doorman. He pierces the rat's body with a pitchfork. Who is going to clean its blood, its red and foaming rat's blood?

≈≈

On October 10, 1980, the earth shook in Algeria. In El Asnam they say that the earth split open, swallowing bodies and eating them alive.

≈≈

It's snowing in Algiers. It's snowing on La Résidence. There is frost on the eucalyptus forest and sheets of ice on the sea. Everything is falling apart.

≈≈

In the city center a man chases children with an ax. He strikes blindly in the crowd amidst the chaos of shopping. He wounds unknowingly. My mother sees everything. She will tell me later. Is that what "to take leave of one's senses" means?

≈≈

wed: locking and bolting the door, not giving out your phone
ber, not putting your name on the mailbox. But you will not be
d of Algerians. You'll be afraid of French people, their violence,
' thirst for blood, and their thirst for stories. You will be afraid
iose vampires, afraid of those who want to know everything,
e sense of everything, understand everything about Algeria's
ery and its situation. They will ask you. They will feed off of you
out ever devouring you, capturing you, or understanding you.
will not know that your body remained behind. It remained in
ria because our history is there. Amine, you already knew about
lren's fragility: my attempted kidnapping, our mothers' pre-
ions and prohibitions. They are your age, and you watch them.
se warriors. They have your eyes, your hair, and your hands. You
hem on the news, watch their expressions; you hear their first
es, their voices. It's as if you're looking at yourself or contem-
ing me. I could have hit you, hurt you, suffocated you. I could
destroyed you with my love. You will feel guilty for not having
anything, not having warned me that everything was simmer-
Little signs and small silences: you knew already that every-
g was unraveling. Like our separation. Remember those years
n you used to dance in Algeria to Boney M., ABBA, and Santana,
e years when you sang with me to the songs of Faïrouz, Idir,
Abdel Wahab. Remember how you used to laugh with me in
ria. You used to dive from the cliffs of Rocher Plat. You used to
bathe in Moretti, at Club des Pins, on Zeralda Beach. You used
alk on the levy of Sidi-Ferruch. You felt alive walking between
Aurès and the Assekrem. You walked across the desert like the
e Prince of the kingdom. You felt alive walking between Bejaïa
Cherchell, Blida and Mostaganem. These spoken landmarks
rehashed by French people. These illustrations. These territo-
of violence.

The foreign television programs are no longer running. I wait for
Le Fugitif, *La Piste aux étoiles*, and the terrifying music of *Les Dossiers
de l'écran*. I wait until midnight, then I count the well-lit electrical
poles that delineate the Mitidja plains.

≈

We can no longer drink water from the faucet. We wash lettuce
and vegetables with cleansing agents. We stock Saïda and Mouza-
ïa crates. We have to wash our hands, take off our shoes, and only
eat cooked food.

≈

I get a violent fever that lasts five days. It's inexplicable. It runs its
course into adulthood then disappears.

≈

I wake up every night, trying to understand what is suddenly hap-
pening. It's like the end of a love affair: little signs that tell us that
the story is drawing to its close. I am often afraid. I walk across the
apartment, wandering and searching. I go all the way to the mirror
at the end of the long corridor. I see an old man with black teeth
wearing a red fez.

≈

It is harder and harder to see you, Amine. You say it's dangerous to
hang around here like this. Even in the garden. Even in your room.
It's dangerous to listen to "Yellow Submarine" so loudly. Your walls
are not thick enough. Your mother has won. But who is the most
dangerous? Me or Algeria? What is the difference? I take everything
from Algeria.

≈

A dream returns. Every night. A nightmare. It's such a powerful
and detailed dream that it wakes me up. It's a prophesy, a rendezvous. My night is dark. My father's hand reaches for my feverish

face, while my mother's offers a glass of ice water. Here comes Rabiâ's extended hand. My sister's words reach me along with her undivided attention and her patience. Here comes Bachir's resuscitated voice. It's this nightly discomfort that will make me leave Algiers every summer. This foreboding, this thick night. To leave, to get some air. To move away from this dream, from this country. Nina has to breathe. Nina is so sensitive. This is my summer vacation. The fire, an assault, enters my bedroom. I know. I know Algeria's future like I knew the earthquake was imminent. I know the blood: it's coming. One must simply look to see the sadness of these closed faces, people's new behaviors. My mother saw it all coming. It will be easy to write, to say it afterward. But in fact all one needs to do is look and listen to Algeria. Algeria, a country so alone, such abandonment, such immense solitude. France's revenge. In my dream, men devour each other. Each man for himself. One against the other. It will no longer be a fight between cats and rats. It will be a lot more serious; there will no longer be any excuses. No more leniency. No more women, no more children, no more old people. War for all. War against all. Bodies are meant to be burned and pillaged, lives to be undone. Algerian life is so precious. I am telling you my dream, Amine. You are afraid of me, still. Your mother was right. You believe in my madness, my extravagance. Yes, I believe I'm a man, but a man who sees, a man who knows. Amine, you're impeded by your childhood. You lack awareness. This dream will inspire writing about my secret. I will write to flee the world, to escape your gaze. To lose Algiers. To lose Algeria. It seems impossible, but it will happen, Amine.

First, I have to leave during the summer. Everything suffocates me here. The sea evaporates with the heat, and nights are difficult. I soak the sheets with my sweat and sleep on the cool tiles, waiting for daylight, trying to avoid the dream by staying up. I have to leave you and bid you farewell, Amine. I will go to my French grandparents' house, where I will encounter another war as I flee the dreams of massacres and heartless persecutions. I have to flee

all the blades that shine in my night. Am
massacres and the violence in Algeria, as
talk to you about it without listening to w
will ask you about Algeria without hearin
want to know. They will get closer to A
skin, your body, and narrating voice. Th
ria. For them it is merely a good deed, a f
say the names of the villages, the roads,
won't really know these women, these
Meanwhile, you will know the intimacy
it's yours as well. You will feel this frighte
ly. No, they won't know the feeling. The
while, though not every night like you do
obsessed as you. You will search in Alger
Algerian radio stations, watch rebroadca
on a road map, look in a road atlas, reme
your friends, your neighbors, and your t
from them. This silence will already be
people will talk to you about this violenc
dering violence that we foresaw. Unknow
the end of our story. You will say: "I kno
because of Nina's dream." They will say
you haven't lived there for a long time, t
and that it's indecent. This is what they'
French and therefore you are saved. You
this now foreign country. France is your
quil. A handsome and calm man." This is
"You don't even look like an Arab; you do
will answer: "But Algerians are not Ara
of their neuroses and fantasies. They inv
get from you. Furthermore, they will say:
status; you're not even a refugee. What d
ing, terror, and that life?" You will be as
being scared on the street. Ashamed of tl

RENNES

I leave Algiers and its scorching summer behind. I leave the eucalyptus grove, La Résidence, Les Glycines, and L'Orangeraie. I leave
my apartment, the white and frozen sea, the Mitidja plains, and the
top of Mount Chréa. I'll be gone for two months. Leaving Algeria is
an ordeal. My departure seems impossible, almost final. This city
gets under one's skin. It is haunting. To leave feels like a betrayal.
The city could take revenge and bring bad luck. To leave is an act of
violence. Algiers permeates everything: the heat, the thick air, the
proliferating smells of burned pine, dried earth, and red sand. It
smells like summer and like death. Mothballs in my winter clothes,
white sheets on the furniture, closed shutters; we straighten out our
bedrooms. Living in Algiers is a constant struggle against the sun. I
leave for summer vacation to breathe, says my mother. To protect my
bronchial tubes, throat, and lungs, to prevent asthmatic bronchitis.
To flee the dream, the announced massacre. The air is stifling here.
It is thick and filled with ashes. It comes from the mountains that
are aflame, creating a red line around the city. I am dressed for the
occasion, this long trip. I am dressed to leave Algiers, myself, and
my real life. Jeans, shorts, terry cloth shirts, flip-flops, and shaggy
hair are okay here, but not in France. I must look presentable, well-
groomed, to make them forget that my father is Algerian and that
I am Algerian too. I have Rabiâ's face and Bachir's skin. Nothing
from Rennes. Nothing but a birth certificate and my French nationality. I try to make them forget my name. Bouraoui: the storyteller's
father. It comes from *abou*, meaning the father, and *rawa*, meaning
to tell a story. I am dressed to stifle Ahmed and Brio, to hide. My
grandmother likes real girls. I must forget that my body is made
for the light, the sand, and the salty winds. I have to make amends:

that's the real reason for this departure, for this forced vacation. I must make amends for my mother. You won't marry an Algerian. My body so soft, so tender, a seduction. Making amends for this story between the French woman and the Algerian student. Making amends for 1962, for independent Algeria. My body confronts the men of the OAS, my eyes watch their moves. My voice rises above their orders. Making amends for this allegiance to Algeria, for my sister and myself born at the Hôtel-Dieu maternity in Rennes. My mother's spoils: her daughters, her treasures exhibited and traded for summer vacation and forgiveness. The daughters of the Algerian son-in-law who speaks excellent French—such small, refined, and well brought up little girls.

I am wearing a thin pair of pants—very girly—a print with little red hearts, like blood stains replicated on a blouse with short, puffed sleeves. A Daniel Hechter suit, an outfit I detest. My costume, my French skin. To leave. To look for my second face but never to find it. To suffer from it. To hold my tongue. One, two, three, viva Algeria![16] To erase my accent. To live in nostalgia, forever missing both my mother and my father. Not to tell anyone that I come from Algeria, that country an unknown land. To hear: "Do you live at Algiers?[17] Do you have a car? Aren't you starving?" In the seventies French people are not yet used to Algerians, mixed marriages, and second-wave immigrants. They are fixated on the Algerian war and on images of the desert, the *fellagha*,[18] and the maquis.

We will be the only girls from Algiers in Brittany on Minhic's huge, ice-cold family beach. My sister and I, two naked and dark bodies, two orphans with our Algerian faces and our French native tongue. Who will know the violence of this secret? We will lie often,

16. "One, two, three" is in English in the original French text.—*Translators*
17. The original sentence in French, "Tu vis en Alger," intentionally uses the incorrect preposition. This emphasizes French people's ignorance: the city of Algiers is confused with the country of Algeria.—*Translators*
18. *Fellagha* are the Algerian partisans who fought against the French during the Algerian War of Independence (1954-1962).—*Translators*

pretending to be foreigners. Two exiles. We will not miss Algeria per se. We will miss the routine of the voices, the faces, the dizzying waves, and the heat. We will lie often, telling about our country, Algeria, our city, Algiers, our desert, Taghit, our beach, Moretti, as if we are trying to be loved by Algeria. But we will know the danger of these places, their violence. We will be the first ones to know, subjected to it before anyone else. We will be rejected and separated from Algeria. Of course it will not be France that we detest; it will be the idea of a certain France, of some families' ingrained habits, limited by their complexity, their complexes, their heritage. French will not be the problem; it is the only language we are able to understand. The beach will not be the problem either or these new first names that we'll need to learn and to call: Rémi, Marion, Olivier — these French names, the opposite of Amine, Feriale, Mohand. The problem resides at the heart of families met by chance on vacation; it's woven into their hatred, their judgments, and their verdicts. Arabs out. The problem lies in their inability to truly love what is foreign, what is different, what is fleeting. It lies in this incompatibility between us and them. My hatred for a certain kind of France comes from the inhumanity of these families, these particular cases, not from the land or its inhabitants. Rather, it comes from a narrow space, intimate and minuscule. A family geography, the place where debts are settled.

To leave Algeria behind and the boredom that comes with summer: the heat, the city's paralysis, and the silence that resembles a fall. It all comes from the sky and the sun. It falls to Earth with the weight of inertia. To leave behind scorching days and burning beaches. To go play elsewhere. To pretend. To wear real shoes, shoes that cover our feet. Not to eat with our fingers. To say "hello" and "thank you." To wear dresses. To remain silent. To go back to the source, the first scream, the first blood in Rennes. I am leaving with my sister. We are going to "breathe" together. To breathe French air, the smell of the lawn, the damp earth, the Channel, and seaweed. To breathe the smell of death in Brittany's cemeteries.

The smell of granite villages, the garden's gates, trimmed hedges, and the gravel alley. The smell of the car seats, brioche and chocolate, the attic, the cellar, and the dental office. The smell of yellow, pink, and blue bedrooms, freshly cut flowers, French food: pork roast and apples, chicken stew, sesame cookies, chitterlings, roasted ham. To breathe fully. The smell of Plage du Pont, Marion's hair. To breathe and to hear their story, the engines of their cars. To hear the jet engines taking us away, the train's doors closing up. The Corail train's glide, its sliding doors, and dining car. This sadness and the smell that permeate my skin, my hands, my clothes. To hear again the voice of the French conductor: "Algiers–Rennes." He knows nothing about Ghardaïa, Timimoun, Djanet. He only works the Le Mans–Vitré–Laval–Fougères line. This is his desert, his world, his universe.

He will not know a thing about the women whose throats have been slit, the children whose bodies have been burned, the slashed bellies, the pierced eyes. No, he will not know a thing about it. Just like he knows nothing about me. He does not know that I wear an Air Algeria pouch around my neck, just in case. He does not know that my entire life weighs on my chest. Yasmina Bouraoui. La Résidence. 63-22-92. Algiers, Algeria. Just like he knows nothing about my Daniel Hechter suit, its color, its form, its fabric, and that I hate having to wear it. Just like he knows nothing about this love that I recover here in Rennes for my mother.

And to hear the sound of the bells again. This is France with its ringing church bells. This mass that I know nothing about, their baptism medallions, their navy blue skirts, and their long hair tied back. These songs, these signs, these prayers, their First Communion: a foreign language. To leave Algiers, the stares of men, the fire, the heat lightning, and the sky. To flee the violence of this earth and to carry it with me, to export it to France, Brittany, Rennes. To Saint-Malo. I am going to war. I take with me my mother's scarf, her smell, her perfume. The silk cloth on my cheek is my weapon. She will join us later. After. At the end of the summer, after the change in our bodies. It is in Brittany that they will grow up, get strong, catch up, compensate for what they lack in that dry country, that savage Algeria, as they say.

To leave and come back in September with a French accent, a slip of the tongue that will dissipate rapidly.

≈

He is on the platform. He is waiting. His whole body, slender and thin, penetrates the premises, this station, the last stop. He sees us but does not come. He stays put in the arrival area. He does not run. He does not come through the crowd. He stands up straight, immobile. He is taller than all the arriving passengers. He is my mother's father, our French grandfather. Above all, he is my mother's father. Her bond. Her Algerian war. He wears a white short sleeved shirt, beige pants, and carries a jacket on his shoulder. Our grandfather does not look his age. His beard is neatly trimmed. He is the only man I know who cuts his beard like this. Nobody does this in Algeria. They have mustaches, long beards, or short beards, but not this clean style cut, the particular sign that singles him out. Our French grandfather. To cut one's beard, to let one's beard grow: it's a performance as well as a sign of recognition. Later they will talk about the full-bearded Algerian fundamentalists, not about these mutton-chops, no. Or they really will be talking about the lamb chops then, the barbecued lamb of the Eid celebration. The slit throats. Not his thin, well-trimmed beard, a ring around his fleshy lips that creates a kind of symmetry in his large, strong face.

We come from Algiers. El Djazaïr. Our skin still burning, we don't trust our new surroundings yet. To watch. To look around us at these men, these women, and this child who follows. We enter the place with the smell of the Corail train on our clothes, the taste of ham sandwiches in our mouths, and the undeniable feeling of being in France.

I am in Rennes. I always fully immerse myself in the places I visit. I belong in the moment, its permanence, its truth. This way I quickly erase everything that happened before. I don't remember anything anymore about the plane, the trip, the flight, the cockpit, the stewardess, her gestures, or her attention. I have wiped out everything already in revenge. Me, I did not want to leave. I am in Rennes, the city of my birth. I don't remember anything anymore about the police, customs, passports, or the lounge reserved for children traveling alone. I will always be a girl traveling alone. At fifteen. At twenty. At thirty-two. Always. I will forever feel this vertigo of solitude as well as this excitement of being alone with my body, my voice. Being self-sufficient, fleeing others, hiding, walking alone. I don't remember anything about the former sheep trail, the rows of palm trees, the el-Harrach River. This mythical road from the Dar el-Beïda airport. I don't remember anything about the faces, the words, the probable tears, the separation, Orly airport, the friend who picks us up at the Montparnasse train station. I no longer know. I have destroyed everything in revenge. I am in Rennes. My life is like this always, exaggerated and extreme. I erase everything so fast, living in the moment. I prefer immediate sensation. This way I accept the force of time. I accept the violence of being here, alive, in Rennes.

I carry my suitcase with both hands. It's a huge suitcase filled with vacation stuff, my Algerian life that I bring along with me. I will always have a big suitcase like all Algerians and like all these foreigners who get off the train, the boat, the plane, encumbered. A full house in their hands, an identity to lift, a family to move and to bring along. All these fragments of memory, these little signs: material lives. Some day they will search these suspect suitcases. Algerians will be parked in the backs of airports, behind hidden doors, in special cells with their particular desks. Gloved hands will search the possessions and the bodies of men, women, and children. These very dangerous Algerian passengers, these human bombs, these people from the war declared terrorists with the sole evidence of their faces, their first names, and their destinations. Benaknoun. Telemny. Cité Saint-Eugène. Very dangerous. Hands up. Claim your suitcase. Whose child is this? What are you doing in France? These foreigners, animals that should be kicked out. They will look for axes, knives, explosives, searching for security purposes, they say, but also to defile and humiliate. The war in Algeria has never stopped; it has hardly changed. The war simply has moved to another place and continues its course. My pain from carrying this too-heavy suitcase is a symptom of this war, which also manifests itself on the face of my older sister, Jami. She suddenly becomes my little sister, with her wounded face. Wearing her red dress, with her dark skin and big green eyes, she leaves with all her stuff, encumbered. She moves forward with all her strength, toward this motionless man, our French grandfather.

≈≈

He is here, huge and strong. He hugs both our bodies. It hurts a bit. It's from all the emotion. His lips on our foreheads, his hands around our shoulders. This surprised expression from finally seeing us after such a long trip. He seems happy with his two granddaughters from Rennes and Algiers, his two kids from the Hôtel-Dieu maternity ward, Jami and Nina, his two loves from now on. Our eyes, our hair, our skin. Could it be that everything disappears with time and gets erased? He asks questions. Jami answers, always, with a different voice, a serious and controlled voice. Yes, we had a good trip. Yes, they are well. Tears come to my eyes. I feel a sudden longing for my life, my friends. This movement, all this agitation, the train cars that get detached in the midst of screams. The smoking engine car. The luggage carts. The porters. The whistles. The travelers who are pushing and shoving. This exhaustion. I hate train stations. I hate trains. They are abrupt like death. They are too close to the earth, this morbid belly waiting to consume all bodies. I prefer airports. Airplanes are closer to the sky, dream life, and the clouds. Trains. Death trains. All these crowds, these long vacations.

As for me, I am on vacation from my Algerian life.

All these screams, flotation devices, fishing nets, and inflatable boats. The sea is not far: Dinard. Saint-Malo. Saint-Lunaire. Saint-

Briac. All these white children run toward the cold sun and the icy waves of Brittany's coast. All these little bodies already dead. These white children, their small torsos, their narrow ribs, their tiny uncovered knees wearing jumpers, Bermuda shorts, blouses, chemises as they say. Their words so very French. I have to lose my accent. They will never know how to jump off the cliffs of Rocher Plat; they are too thin and white. They cling to their mothers, aided and safe. They live in this calm and rich country, in this profusion. They are able to sleep. But I keep searching, my bags always packed. I run faster than other kids. I am active and full of life. These kids seem ill.

All these stares on me, my Daniel Hechter suit, my girl pants. Eyes on my suitcase, my Air Algeria pouch, my dark skin and golden eyes. The eyes of a snake, a viper with horns. Nina, the venomous poison. He says: "My little granddaughters." He makes up for the time of the war, all this lost time. I shed tears. It's my stance against French Algeria. Against France for French people. Against Brittany that invades and erases me with its unquestioning ways. Brittany, with so many white bodies that run toward the trains, their families reunited for summer vacation. They all have the same words, the same images: the beaches, Mickey Mouse clubs, walks on the jetty, the evening waffle with chocolate or powdered sugar, fresh sand under their feet, and the sea that retreats so far. The great tide, then the equinox tide. The catamaran teacher, sailboard lessons, and the small, well-organized life of summer's cycle.

This little death lying in wait, the death of these petit bourgeois families. Do they know about Tipaza and Bérard? Will they have enough love to hear the stories of a drowning Algeria? Enough time? Enough interest? Who will truly look at the decapitated body of this child? Who? My grandfather? My grandmother? Marion, my French friend? Who besides the mother of the child? Who will know the danger of night falling on the Mitidja plains? The danger of the Baïnem forest, the deserted roads, and the false checkpoints? The danger in the slightest noise, not this brouhaha or this swarming train station: their words, their accents, and their laughter. The noise of metal wheels on tracks, a crash. All of a sudden I am an orphan. Orphan and free.

≈≈

Everything separates me from my Algerian life. Everything: this noise, this train station, the rushing passengers, and my grandfather, who does not mention Algiers, its beaches, the sun, or the scalding heat. He remains silent on the ever so difficult Algerian life, the future of Algerians, their suffering, the shortages, the scarcity, and the instigation of violence. He says nothing at all. He asks about my father, his latest missions, his 'round-the-world trips, his work and professional responsibilities. Fortunately, my father is not a laborer. He is not an immigrant worker, one of those who needed quick shelter in barracks, in shantytowns, or in Sonacotra[19] villages that had neither water nor electricity. Those who have been humiliated, ghettoized, and isolated. Those who were prevented from getting an education for fear of rebellion, who were exploited, brought back from Algeria like a commodity. Strong hands, workers' flesh. Men first and later their wives, brought back like packages by mail, by these overcrowded boats. Such a dehumanizing experience. This shame, accepted and recognized reluctantly. This French shame. No, my father is an economist: all the better. He travels a lot: whew! He is an educated Algerian: bravo! A high-ranking government worker: even better! He then asks about my mother, her health, her life, and her new job, in a serious tone of voice. His daughter. He calls her Méré. I have never known why. Méré. *Mare. Mare Nostrum.* Our Mother Sea. My mother, there in the Mediterranean waters.

Past the stairs at the Rennes train station, past this metallic noise that seems to follow me everywhere, past the white children's stares my grandfather's car is waiting for us. His pride, his chariot, his

19. Sonacotra (Société Nationale de Construction pour les Travailleurs) is an agency created in 1957 that is responsible for housing Algerian immigrant workers in France. —*Translators*

little sin. Only American cars: Ford, Buick, Chevrolet. Their large doors, their shiny wheels, and their finishes. A single front seat and a back seat that fits five people. A leather steering wheel, automatic transmission, large pedals for an easy ride, iridescent color, streamlined hood, and a family-size trunk: the scale of the United States. Cars that fit him. Here, he can unfold his long legs, use his large hands to steer. His strong and muscular dentist's hands. The hands of an angry father. Two little Algerian girls sitting in the large American car. It is so funny. From Moretti to Buick, from Algiers Beach to the five-passenger back seat. From Dar el-Beïda airport to the Thabor house. Ford, Buick, Chevrolet. I believe I threw up in each one of them.

≈≈

He says: "Tomorrow I will check your little teeth."
Lucky teeth, Nina.
Patients, colleagues, assistants.
Dental office.
To go to the contending team.
Cloves soothe the pain.
The fish tank in the waiting room keeps the fear away.

≈≈

At first I hear the little dog; she barks behind the door of the house. A tiny short-haired dachshund, so lovable with her small, expressive eyes. A smell of hazelnuts behind her ears. On the street she knits with her little paws. She is a real hot-water bottle at night. She understands everything, this little barking dog. Everything except Algeria. Everything except this strange trip, this uprooting. Everything except my sadness and the stares on my short hair. Nina is a tomboy, a failed girl. Nina, if this keeps up you will grow a weenie or a goatee.

Be very careful of her little heart. She's so fragile, so moving, just like a child. She recognized you right away. It's incredible! Beware of cars! She is so happy that she jumps up my calves and licks my legs. I will whisper in her ear and tell her that in Algeria we don't like dogs, that we stone them to death in memory of the war. The French army used them against Muslims. Since then Algerians are terrified of dogs. It is humiliating to be devoured by an animal. One never forgets.

My grandmother appears happy on the porch of the great white house. It is summer vacation. My little ones, my children, you must be starving. All dark and sun-tanned. Nina, the spitting image of her father. I set you up on the second floor, in the room with the boat-bed. It's my favorite bedroom. I added a small bed for Nina. Me, I know that I will sleep right next to my sister's body, feeling her skin and taking in her smell. My protection against the night, the noise of the creaky wooden floor, and the twelve midnight rings of the old grandfather clock. Nina, this blouse is nice. My girl suit. I got a doctor's appointment for tomorrow morning, and you will drop by the dental office in the afternoon. We will check everything before we leave for Saint-Malo. Come see the garden; it is magnificent. The ivy has grown a lot; now it covers the communal wall. The palm tree is still there. Palm trees are so resistant, but you know that already. Where has the turtle gone? I made dumplings for dinner. Do you like that?

I am going to look for the turtle near the rosebushes. I know the garden of the house in Rennes quite well. It smells good. Summer is my favorite season; it is Algeria all over again. The sunlike smell induces vertigo. Its hot air is like arms embracing me. I feel the presence of the sea so close when my eyes are closed. I became very familiar with the garden of the house in Rennes one winter. Every morning I got used to the smell of the earth, the grass being watered, the hissing sound of the revolving sprinkler, the gravel path, the well-trimmed hedges, the small kitchen stairs, and the two rabbit cages. Holding my white rabbit, his warm ears between my hands, I look out the great bay windows in the living room and notice the place where the little dog falls asleep quietly. The smell of France permeates everything, even summer, the sun, and the heat. I feel so far from Algeria all of a sudden; it seems that I have forgotten it. I take advantage of this change of scenery. I feel free because it is still daylight. Because I am dizzy from traveling. Because nothing is real. I will go back for sure. This is a dream. My ability to adjust is an escape from reality. I am here without really being here. The turtle is on its back with its rough legs and prehistoric head. I put it right side up and save its life.

I am in Rennes, my birth place. My ears ring. I am in Rennes, in the house of my mother's childhood, the place of her history. Her bedroom is on the top floor directly beneath the roof. In springtime she must have read here in the grass. She listened to jazz, wrote poems, and studied law here. She must have thought right here on this bench, thought of what she had to say: How will I say it? How will I announce it? How will I tell them? How will I explain?

So, I met a guy, a university student. He is Algerian, well, French Muslim, as they say. I love him and want to marry him. He will come here, to the small blue sitting room, to ask for my hand. He lives in the dorms. Yes, his whole family is in Algeria, in the East. Don't you want to know? It is her solitude I feel, then her fear. This huge fear of having to announce something serious: saying, speaking, affirming oneself. It is so difficult knowing before other people do and anticipating their reactions. It creates frightening fears and gives a stomachache. Such bad news in the middle of war. To kiss the enemy, desire him. To make peace before others do through the body: to mix and have children. I feel this fear. It is still here in this garden, under my feet, in my body burning with the heat of the sun. Tomorrow I will go to the doctor to check my Algerian life, just in case. Blood, hearing, bones, reflexes. To inspect the body, search, detect any signs of nutritional deficiency. Yes, sir, we eat enough vegetables, meat, and dairy. Blood tests, x-rays, and a stethoscope to check that all is well after living in that country, that land, North Africa. The French health system takes over, appropriating and searching our bodies; it penetrates from head to toe. Nina has webbed toes, the middle ones. Does she suffer from it? No, she walks normally. But yes, I do suffer from it. I am ashamed of it and often bandage them. Where does it come from? Her French side. She has bad posture, doctor. Isn't it scoliosis? No. What about her fevers? Is that malaria? No. Isn't she too small for her age? No.

Tomorrow they will examine me although I am completely healthy.

With nightfall comes mourning for the day past. It's the death of everything: the sun, the memory of the sea, the garden, roses, raspberries, and happy life. The terrible distance that separates me from my people extends like an infinite bridge and endures like an injustice. My voice does not carry all the way there. Who can hear me? I have my mother's scarf in my hand; my open suitcase filled with vacation stuff sits in the room with the boat-bed. A pink bathroom, a desk, a dresser, a fireplace, and a large mirror: it is Fanfan's bedroom. I am in my mother's house, the house of her childhood, and all of a sudden my life reflects hers like a mirror. In one night I replace my mother's features: my face over her face, my voice over her voice. I go up to the top floor. I look for her books. Her letters. Her notebooks. Her notes. Her law school notes. To seek. What is written. What remains. What binds. What reveals. To seek my father's first name written secretly, the evidence. To verify my mother's existence here, in this place, in this house in Rennes. Her toddler years, her first tracings of the alphabet, her communion photo. With her smooth and well-defined heart-shaped face, light-colored eyes, skin so soft, she is all in white, a candle in her hand. This beautiful face used to avoid mirrors. Who undermined your self-confidence, Méré? Who did not adore you as you adore me?

Her first communion candle. What was her wish? To leave. To travel. To study elsewhere. To go as far as possible, on the other side of the sea.

Méré, such a different child, so stubborn.

Her house with its hardwood floors in each bedroom, a large staircase, statues, paintings, her portrait, a grandfather clock that rings on the hour and half hour, accounting for time. My mother,

Méré, also nicknamed "Little Mother" by her sisters, took good care of the little ones, protecting them, explaining girl issues, life matters. Méré, Mary, Maryvonne, her intelligence, her softness. She replaced her parents, took care of the little ones while they were at the dental office with patients, pulling teeth, polishing, filling, and healing them in the end. Méré. Your father's key in the keyhole, his authority, his strength, pliers in his dentist's hands. Méré, sensitive, rebellious, and independent. Méré's bedroom. Go to sleep or bad Sidi will come to get you. Sidi, the werewolf from the former colonies. Méré, the only one who loves an Algerian, the only one in the family. Maryvonne's case: the only one with multiracial children, who left her youth behind for Algeria, the country of men. Méré, little mother who will accompany Fanfan, her younger sister, till the end. She will hold her hand for a long time and place a rose on her body. Fanfan, the youngest sister, who worried so much. Fanfan, I brought you a croissant and a small chocolate pastry.

Fanfan will play so often with us.

For a long time I will carry my mother's childhood with me like an heirloom, like a wound that my happy life must erase, like an injustice I have to bear. A childhood in limbo, a secret and worrisome childhood, a childhood in danger. I will carry it for a long time to alleviate my mother's pain, to heal her, and help her love herself. For a long time I will take her fears: fear of silence, fear of the night, and fear of accidents. Anxiety, as they say, a catastrophic life. Was it more than the German bombs dropped at night near the house? Was it more than the Stars of David drawn on every storefront? This violence, this denunciation. Was it more than the blood of this bullfight in Spain? Who caused the fear? Who instilled it in you, Méré?

With the physical strength of a taut body, a body that wants to believe and does not want to give up, Méré will wait for love, proof of love, for a very long time. Stubborn, strong-willed, and combative Méré, a little soldier. For love, love, love. Love that becomes a prayer, supplicating love expressed in her eyes, her letters, and the offering of her children every summer. Nevertheless, silence will take over. Silence about the massacres, the suffering in Algeria, and our new life. A silence that spreads contagiously, a real disease, a plague, an epidemic. Silence on every mouth. The silence of France. The silence of the whole world. Silence about Algeria, burned bodies, dismembered bodies, disemboweled bodies, this incredible puzzle of ripped open flesh. Absolute silence about this human disorder, silence about man's future. Silence about his true nature.

Fish dumplings in the huge Thabor house kitchen. It's really important not to waste food. How many Russian roulette turns? How many dental fillings? We need to keep this in mind. One learns very early on to finish one's plate and to think about young, starving Africans. Algeria is an African country. Algeria is a French overseas department. Algiers is hemmed in by the Mediterranean Sea like the Seine River winding through Paris.

The shutters are closed, but the windows remain open. I hear people passing by, slowly, so close to our table, our feast. The rhythm of their steps alone is a sign of summer, a slow dragging life. So is the sound of their noisy mopeds, an escapade. Their laughter, the warm air that comes through the wood of the shutters, a bowl of water for the little dog, a wine bottle on the table, bread, cheese, fruit, and desserts. Yes, they love us despite this complicated life, our Algerian life. Two months vacation, isn't that proof? In the background I hear voices on television, commercials, as they are now called. I memorize them. In Algiers, Le Français cinema is the only place that plays an ad for Selecto, an Algerian soda. My grandfather, his voice, his hands: "Empty your plate, my child."

I am so far from everything, suddenly.

Soft white cheese with sugar. Jami tells us about the beach, the sun, her girlfriends. Me, I have nothing to say. Tomorrow my body will be examined. Tomorrow they will find Ahmed and possibly Brio. Tomorrow I will go through Rennes, the city that belongs to the lovers from 1960. Tomorrow, my x-ray. My silence, a shield against the voices and the laughter on the street. Still more mopeds. Clandestine life. To escape, to dance, to enjoy our vacation. I drown in my soft white cheese, thick milk, a sweet taste. Amine. Cherchell. Amine. Tipaza. These wet bodies. All this sun. These salt crystals on the skin of Algerian divers. This strength. My naïve and romantic life. Here, I am under surveillance: my back, my eyes, my teeth. Two foreigners. To be checked inside out. Where did childhood go all of a sudden? Death has arrived; it's on the skin of these dark bodies still burning from the sun.

I hear the voice of France resonating on local television: peasants from Brittany, the Rance Dam, the Bigouden dance, and the Kouign-aman recipe. This life closed in on itself, this very French France, this small fish bowl, this folklore that I detest just like I detest Algerian folklore. Wicker baskets, the Southern Cross, pottery plates, children's burnouses, kerosene lamps, and flying carpets. This dangerous folklore, cultural identity reduced to a small piece of land in need of protection and defense. They have raised barbed wire around their folklore to protect it from strangers, the speed of life, progress, and invasion.

The phone rings: Yes, they have arrived okay. These distant voices, barely real, so far away in the deep reaches of the night, stolen by this new life, our French summer. But no, I am not crying. Yes, it is from being tired. Tomorrow will be better. Yes, I know that you think about me. Communication between Algiers and Rennes is difficult. The lines are always busy.

≈

Night is truly the death of everything; it is the death of days past, this trip, the train, and the bygone Algerian voices. Night claims everything. It is an invasion. Only the house stands glowing in the night. It is as if I had never left it. It becomes my house with its wooden scent, the clock's ring, and the water running in the pipes. I hear steps near the bedroom, small steps. A night watch to check that the shutters are closed, the oven is turned off, the garden gate is shut, and to check that the little dog sleeps in her basket and that the two girls are in bed. Small steps that shake the whole house. There are four of us. Two against two. Four of us hear and count the rings: eleven o'clock, eleven thirty, midnight, twelve thirty. I am the only one who stays up almost until daybreak. Night is an ocean; it seems eternal. Night is the enemy of children. It is an adversary, a man who persecutes women. Night heightens fragilities. Night is deadly.

Tomorrow, daylight. Tomorrow, life. Tomorrow, the examination of our little burning bodies. Tomorrow, hot chocolate. Tomorrow, crêpes from Brittany. Tomorrow, the little dog's happiness when she slides between the sheets with her hazelnut smell, her little paws, her belly always wanting to be kneaded, caressed, scratched, her pink and busy tongue, her eyes, such intelligent eyes. She understands everything, this little dog. Everything. Be careful, you hurt her, Nina. You are too rough. Slowly, go slowly. Little dogs are fragile. She has a rapidly beating heart, a little head, and soft pads. A dog is a child who does not talk. A dog is a woman who does not cry. A dog is a man who does not abandon.

A little dog is fragile. It can die of a head cold.

With night comes the idea of death, immense and precise. A rendezvous. For a long time before going to sleep, I repeated to myself: I don't want to die, I don't want to die, I don't want to die. A simple idea becomes reality for Algerian children. The biggest massacres will take place at night. Night is a mask. Night erases all shapes. Night suppresses witnesses and drives people crazy as well. It is not reality any more. It is another life, a faceless life, smooth and intangible. Night is a drowning. The night of the assault. The blood and the fire of the night. It is then that they will take the villages. It is then, in the dark, so as to remain blind to their action, that they will kill. Relentlessly.

Then I understood that it was about something else, about another fear. Not the fear of death per se, not the projection of my own disappearance. The fear takes on another meaning, another resonance, another tone. "I don't want to die" means I don't want to be abandoned. "I don't want to die" means I want to be loved, always. "I don't want to die" means I don't want to separate, I don't want to disengage. "I don't want to die" means I am merged and want to stay put. It is not the fear of death per se—it is the loss of the connection, first a break and then amnesia.

My fear of death takes root at this very moment, during this summer night. This feeling of abandonment will follow me, but night and death are not what matter most. No, they are not. Life is what scared me; life's vertigo is what terrified me. That's why I hid behind others and later behind my writing (beautiful but difficult, they'll say always, like an echo).

Some day, having summoned all of my strength, I will find my place in life, and they will know who I truly am. Nina is a droll and funny girl.

Droll and funny.

The idea of death creeps in with the fear of rejection. It might be unfounded, but the feeling is there like a wasp's sting, a pinch, a sensation that comes with the silence of the night. The idea of death comes with always feeling different, not fitting in, not walking straight, being in the margins and feeling like an outsider, confined within myself. Alone. Not being a part of the social order after all. My face, my body that has to be checked, my accent, light but recognizable, especially with the T. My Steve McQueen walk. Is it a scoliosis, doctor? No, it's from *The Thomas Crown Affair*. Steve without Faye, Steve's spirit, Steve's desire for a girl's body. My haircut is too short, way too short, like Stone's.[20] My violent games, my muscular thighs, my swimmer's shoulders: the entire cliffs of Rocher Plat that shaped my body. Dense. My piercing gaze that can set fires, that witnesses and denounces. My gaze, my sole weapon; I will use it often to hurt, to devour, and finally to love. My mirror-gaze on numerous French families that I encounter by chance, their words, their great discussions, and their political positions.

20. Stone is a French singer from the seventies.—*Translators*

These people who say without thinking, without doing it on purpose, supposedly: "rat," "kike," "negro," "faggot," "sand nigger." It's automatic, a mechanism of words within the language. These people whom I don't know and who always say afterward: "I am not talking about you." They add: "It's the wine—red wine does me in." How obscene.

The idea of death will come from these people, whom I run into in France, these unknown people who violate my life. These French people speaking to the little Algerian girl will want to educate themselves; they will want to know. The idea of death will come from their questions, repeated endlessly. Do you get along with your French grandparents? Do you have a boyfriend? Amine? Is that a first name? Is it always hot there? And what about the poverty? Is it stunning? Like in Morocco or in Tunisia? Hardly visible to tourists? No? There are no tourists in Algeria? Really? So its poverty must be dreadful, then: no vacation clubs, no new constructions, no beach resorts. That's truly horrible. Isn't it brutal? And you, what are you in fact? French or Algerian? We prefer to call you Nina instead of Yasmina. Nina is convenient; it sounds Spanish or Italian. This way we don't have to justify our choice of friends.

≋

I feel love that comes with morning. It appears with birdsongs, the little dog under our sheets, and the voice of my grandmother opening the shutters. One more beautiful day. It's summer in France. It's a strange love, somewhat brutal. But what crime are we talking about? Am I responsible for having this face, these eyes? Am I responsible for having this name? I made an appointment for Ms. Djemilla and Ms. Yasmina Bouraoui at 3:00 p.m. What crime is there in forcing them to spell, enunciate, open their mouths wide, and speak loudly enough to be heard by all? Letter by letter, B-o-u-r-a-o-u-i. No, not Baraoui or Bouraqui. It is not that complicated! Bouraoui from *rawa* that means to tell a story, and *Abi* that signifies father. Arabic names are family prisons. One is always "the son of" with Ben or "the father of" with Bou. Masculine family prisons.

What's my crime? Being the daughter of the lovers from 1960. My sole presence, my gaze, my voice, and my identity preserve that moment in time. Putting salt in the wound, dwelling on that terrible period of the war. The OAS. The FLN. The attacks: a couple, two teachers, their throats slit; French women sitting in an outside café, their bloody skirts after the bomb's explosion, their mangled legs. We were so scared of Algerians, the maquis. Resistance fighters. We were scared of their too dark faces, their almond-shaped eyes that stretch during the day and become thin lines when night falls. A night filled with incensed eyes — the night of massacres.

I feel love in my grandmother's hands that wash me, love all over my body, love in the soft voice that says: "It's funny how your whole body is dark, but the soles of your feet are white." I love her rose-scented soap. Her fingers discover me. You have grown up a bit in spite of everything. Wait, I will rinse your hair. Love, loads of toothbrushes, toothpaste, baking soda paste, love with these presents, love atop the kitchen table: a gargantuan breakfast of brioches, chocolate, bread, and crêpes. Nina, I bought the crêpes you like. And love later, from my grandfather, for my books. Is it love or pride? Is it love or forgiveness? Is it love or devouring? It is most certainly love, my mother will say.

Who could have imagined in 1960 my sister and me, here in the kitchen of the Thabor house with the precious little dog against my legs, sitting near the Aga, the enormous oven? My bare feet on the blue tiles. Blue like the sky of the city of Rennes, less blue than the Algerian sky, less deep and less sad as well. It's not a drowning kind of blue; it's a blue that does not bring you down. Rennes is a free city; its sky does not carry the despair of the Algiers sky. Who could have thought this possible? And prior to that, after the Allies' victory, when they returned to the house that had been confiscated by the German army. Who could have imagined this scene? Two little multiracial girls, their mouths smeared with Poulain chocolate. Rachid's daughters sleeping in the house, going to the garden, climbing upstairs, inspecting the top floor, and searching for signs of my mother's life. Her philosophy notes, her civil law notes, her unchanged handwriting: an intelligent student, careful and neat. Bolting down the stairs, playing in the house where German officers used to live, where they took over during the war, yet another war. With the Krauts, one had to walk straight. The German officer was not joking, I am told. Germany-France-Algeria: the war machine. In the small blue sitting room everything is blue: the sofa, the curtains, the wall-to-wall carpet, the bibelots, the velvet cushions. Blue like the Algerian sky. The sitting room is a little boudoir where important matters are discussed and announcements are made. To confess. The little sitting room is where dramas and confessions take place. Every house has a private room, a little geographical retreat reserved for whispers, anger, and sadness.

I brought you together today in the little blue sitting room to announce that . . . The blue sitting room where Rachid asked for Maryvonne's hand, an act of courage. Wearing a nice black suit, black tie, and white shirt, he looked impeccable, fortunately. My father's elegance, his good taste, his sweaters, his shirts, his pants on his very thin body. He speaks French very well, without an accent. He studied at the École normale d'instituteurs in Constantine, in French Algeria. He graduated from Vannes high school. "The Rare Bird" was his nickname. He studied economics at the University of Rennes. That is where he and my daughter met, in the midst of the Algerian war. Our son-in-law, who used to sing to our daughter: "Spring without Love is not Spring." And she would blush, standing at the top of the stairs of the university. These are the relationships that everyone talks about, a new kind of gossip: French female students fall in love with these men and sometimes with sub-Saharan Africans as well. These couples are mocked at school; they get insulted and sullied. But what would Rabiâ have thought of these students' racist jokes? Their insults? Wog, sand nigger, rat. Rabiâ, my father's mother: so soft, so tender, she who had lost Amar already. What would his mother have said, if she had known? Come back, my son, come back. These words about Rachid, my father who is falsely protected by his intelligence, his grades, his education, and his awards. The love of my mother won't budge despite the students' chants. *Radidja la mouquère.*[21] Despite the gazes, the comments. Despite this man who will refuse to sell him a paper. Despite anger from each and every one, their hysteria. Despite the blue sky. And me? What is my role in this story? What do I do with this knowledge? How could I not want revenge? How could I not want to slap the daughter of this reactionary lawyer whom I will meet twenty-five years later?

21. *Radidja la mouquère* is a racial slur. —Translators

Yes, I will want revenge, just like those whom they will call beurs[22] later. The word *Arab* will no longer be acceptable in France. One will say *beur* and even *beurette*.[23] This will become a political issue. These words will replace the terrifying designations — Algerians, Maghrebians, North Africans — words that certain French people will no longer be able to pronounce. *Beur* is playful, and it conveniently puts down an entire generation as well. Neither completely French nor completely Algerian, a generation of wandering people. Nomads and ghost children, these prisoners preserve memory like a fire and hold onto history like an heirloom. They remember hatred like one remembers a unique voice. They burn with desire for revenge. I will have this strength as well, this desire to destroy, go for the kill, denounce, and break free. My sheer strength is restrained, a demon that will surface in writing. The self is not what counts. One can always heal, take care of oneself, dress the wounds caused by other people's hatred. Our parents' memory is what counts. Their suffering, their humiliation, our crib. The context that was awaiting us, all that was said and done; our parents' transmitted wounds are our inheritance. The stares they get in France, in Algeria, then again in France — all of this is what will feed the desire for revenge. One day, standing at the 21 bus stop, I hear a woman say while looking at my father: "There are too many Arabs in France, way too many. And on top of that, they take our buses." Her words and my silence. Too paralyzed to respond and scream: "This man is my father. Re-

22. In *verlan*, a kind of slang that creates words by reversing syllables, *Beur* is the phonetic pronunciation of the word *Arabe* reversed. It refers to the French-born descendants of North African immigrants. — Translators
23. *Beurette* is the feminine of *Beur*. — Translators

spect him or I will curse you. Respect him or I will hit you. Respect him or I will kill you. And he is not just my father; he is also a man. By despising him, it is life itself that you hold in contempt." But nothing came, only my silence. My father and my silence. Scared or simply used to it, he does not say anything either. He will remain in Algiers for increasingly longer periods of time: his solution. As for me, I will be terribly hurt by this woman's words, wounded to the point of silence.

Then it will become routine to hear these sorts of comments. These words will catch like small forest fires spreading all over Paris like traps to avoid or mines to steer clear of. In the streets, in restaurants, in the subway as I walk by I hear a woman's fleeting comment: "Look at them run, those loitering rascals." At the supermarket with my sister and Sophia, another woman stares at us: "We must get rid of them, send them back to their country, exterminate them." Sophia's eyes, her child's eyes. Rage, once more. Nausea, once again. Too paralyzed to respond, my skin blushes, my heart beats, my belly cramps as if I had just been punched. Mute in spite of my violent desire, I do not have access to words. No, I am not afraid. No, I am not a coward. My silence confirms the expression *to be wracked with pain*.[24] And in the Porte Maillot shopping mall this young man who looks like my father: "There goes one. He is an Arab. Yes, he is one of them." Again, my father's silence. *Wracked with pain*. And behind the Montparnasse cemetery: "Hey, Rachel! Hey, Sarah! Hey, bitch!" And outside the Bon Marché department store: "So here is Cohen, Benguigui, or maybe even Abdulsomethingorother." And my silence, again. Small vipers now wrapped around my neck: "You are not like the others." Or: "You don't look like one; you could even pass for Italian." And then: "Really? You have a friend whose name is Yasmina? You?" And my silence as always, because my voice means nothing. It escapes like the wind. Of course, I was not supposed to respond. Still, I did find an answer.

24. This expression is in italics in the original text. —*Translators*

I will make it public. Better yet, I will write and expose their hatred in a book. I write, and someone will recognize himself, find herself pathetic. They will remain voiceless, drowned in silence, wracked with pain.

≋

Without an accent, the young French Muslim asks for my mother's hand in the little blue sitting room and thus enters every family's tradition of hushing and keeping secrets. The blue of the sky, the blue of words. My mother leaves the house to live with him. It is difficult, but they hang on, never asking for anything. Their friends are on their side, teachers, Algerian students, Marie-France, a long-standing ally who will accompany them forever. She will know, and she will talk about them openly. My father receives the Best Student Award in France: one thousand francs; it is quite a bit at the time. He is followed on the street, a shadow behind him, a manhunt in the midst of war. This is unbearable. Good citizens ask to send him back to his country, the best student at the University of Rennes. The request is denied.

After the ceremony at city hall, my parents celebrate their wedding with their friends in a small restaurant in Rennes. Two dissidents, they have the entire world in their hands; they also hold its silence. It was easy, though, for their friends to help, applaud, and embrace them. But obviously he left too soon, feeling angry, maybe. After independence, French Muslims became Algerian. They also became clandestine, aliens, unemployed, and penniless. So he left quickly to look for an apartment in the scorching heat of his country, braving the Algerian hardship.

It was like swimming across the ocean.

And he came back with the keys to an apartment, finally a home for his so-tired wife, for his daughters, his three loves—what counts the most in the world, his beauties. Yes, my father came back despite the rumors.

And we all left in an Air France Caravelle jet airplane, Rennes–

Paris–Algiers. I was suspended, hanging in a hammock, holding on, just in case. I did not even cry; I have always liked the sky, its color, clouds, turbulences, and purity—an immense secret that penetrates.

It was easy to love our son-in-law; he was unlike other Algerian men. But there was not enough time; he left suddenly, too soon. He went there, looking for an apartment for his family in Algeria, that complicated and far away country where postal services do not work and phone lines are bad. We believed he would never come back from that country, where all administrative formalities must be approved by God: *Inch Allah*. North Africa, with its men in baggy pants, its veiled women, its brutal language, and our little granddaughter. White people have always been treated with more indulgence; they have not been subjected to power struggles or conflicts. Yes, it is unfair, but back then it was difficult to open up, to learn, to wait, to get to know each other. We did not know how. It was wartime, and it was asking too much of this typical French family. A family like any other, beyond reproach. A family that goes to work and votes in every election since time immemorial.

≈≈

We left France like we left Algeria, quickly and disorderly. We left as if threatened by indifference and by silence. We left with the persistent and obsessive feeling of being undesirable, homeless, precariously balanced over the void, endlessly moving and fleeing despite ourselves. It's my mother's second one-way trip, a simple return for my father, and a first for my sister and me. Standing on the stairs after disembarking the plane, we feel the Southern wind drying our lips, its fire scorching our bodies like an assault. The pleasure of the burning earth, the smell of palm trees and jasmine. The stares behind customs' glass door in the noisy Dar el-Beïda airport terminal, the speed of cars on the former sheep trail, the rows of palm trees—everything is new to us. We find the little apartment in the Gulf neighborhood and our new life, warm and swarming with people. We had to leave France, and no one helped us or extended a hand. No one. We left for Algeria, a newly independent country—a country soon to be rebuilt by Algerians. The land of grand illusions. The land of Algerian students recently trained in France and the United States. All this grey matter, these workers and idealists headed for Algeria—a fragile land battered with hatred, an exhausted land.

≋

Such fine hands and clean fingernails, the hands of a pianist; this brain, such a brilliant student. We accepted this high-ranking government official despite his elongated face and his anxiety. We will take the girls with pleasure, really. Anything you want. As you please. Every summer, so that they can breathe. It's too bad the summer in Algeria is so humid. That's bad for the body, especially the respiratory system, our inherited weakness. Jami and Nina, so sweet. It was the war. It was fear. We did not know anything, and we imagined the worst then. It is still out of our control sometimes, even now. But we are like everyone else. Who has never had a bad thought, felt moody, or said a bad word? We can't control everything, even if we regret it afterward. That's how it is, but we must be careful. For the girls, these kids who have never been children. You see it in their eyes, their frozen eyes—eyes that pierce you and undress you. Eyes that interrogate and forgive. They never talk about it; it's taboo. They never mention it, but beware of the youngest one, the one who tells unbelievable stories, scary stories. She has great talent and will write terrifying books later. Writers are dangerous people. They are obsessed with truth, their own truth. Writers are childish; they report, they tattle, they cannot keep anything to themselves. One should not socialize with them. They force you to lie, to dissimulate, and defend yourself later.

These kids have never been children because it is difficult to live with the feeling of not having been loved by everyone from the start. The feeling is immediate and instinctual. Later it will change my vision of the world, haunting and consuming me. After being subjected to the hateful gaze of other people on my skin and my face it will become difficult to love myself. It will be difficult not to hate the world, not to want to withdraw.

≋

Yes, it was easy to love Rachid, says my great-grandmother, sometimes rolling her Rs in a loud voice, an age-old voice from the past century. The adorably innocent voice she uses to call her dog, Jasmine. She is a black, medium-size French poodle. Jasmine, come eat; here, Jasmine. Heel. Finish your plate, Yasmina, says a small, nonexistent voice. Here, no one calls me Yasmina. They have forgotten this name, my first name, the name on my birth certificate, the name from the Hôtel-Dieu hospital, my Arabic first name, such a pretty name. It is the name I will use later, when girls I meet in the din of the night ask me, wanting to know. It is the name I must constantly and carefully pronounce, the one that makes me a foreigner in Paris. Jasmine. It's a coincidence that no one notices, except for me, but it is not important. I understand. I am not scared of dogs. Jasmine is a good name for a poodle. It's like swapping human features for dog traits, her soulful eyes, her emotional yapping sounds, and the fragrance of jasmine flowers on her curly coat.

My great-grandmother never pronounces the word *Arab*. Never. Neither does she utter the word *Algerian*, ever. She loves us, I believe. Truly. She often watches us after our doctor's appointments. The following day is a celebration. After the meticulous exam, she invites us to lunch: chicken roast with potatoes that melt in the mouth. The little dog—a curly poodle found at the SPCA—barks while the food is cooking; he is overexcited, and we can't pet him. My darling. My little love. My crazy love. He runs in the small apartment cluttered with bronze and marble statues, terra-cotta objects, cast bodies, sculpted faces, immobile women's busts, women made of stone and their stone breasts, black and shiny bodies that I stare at for a long time. These, along with a collection of pocket watches, small clocks, and paintings by the dozen, are presents from her husband, an ocean liner captain. Travel souvenirs from such a good and generous man, a true lover.

He loved my father. Yes, he loved him. I don't remember his face anymore. I no longer remember his hands or hear his voice. I don't remember. I just know my mother's bond with this man, her grandfather from Saint-Malo. This sailor showered his wife with perfumes and clothes. He knew the sea, its reefs. He had traveled to foreign countries, had learned other languages, and had met all kinds of people. He knew the power of the waves, the wind, the sun, and the moon, his only light in the dark night.

I like my great-grandmother's apartment, its organized chaos and surplus of objects. Like Ali Baba's cave it recreates the Orient in France, bringing a bit of enchantment here in Rennes. A whiff of enchantment in this small modern building lined with green and narrow alleys, this small residence so different from La Résidence with its kitchen, sitting room, and bedroom. Her large hands, her jutting fingernails, always impeccably done, her thick hair, her loud voice, my great-grandmother. Guerlain on her skin, an opossum coat in the winter, long and sculpted legs, her abdominal workouts, her strength and endurance; she is almost a hundred years old, like her mother was before her. Her Christmas presents, Lanvin chocolate shells for each grandchild, a whole tribe. Her life is a performance with dramatic entrances: My son, my love. Her fingers sometimes pinch Jami in the big American car, just like that for no apparent reason—or maybe to demand her silence, the silence of a child who does not say anything. This child looking at the street from behind the window asks what she is doing there and begins to get scared of life and death. Silence. On principle. Showing respect to elders. Her hand is still resting on my forehead after I walk into an electrical post. Rubbing alcohol. No, it does not hurt. You will have a bump. She loves my mother, never showing any contempt. Never. Nothing. This actress takes us to the Maurepas public garden with her black, medium-size French poodle, whose name is Jasmine.

Her little dog, her companion, her little girl. Such solitude with a little dog. The silence between the two of them. A deadly silence. The miniature poodle finally grew. She knew in advance; she followed my great-grandmother and let herself die. My great-grandmother lets me watch television despite the beautiful weather outside; it is no big deal, we will go out after Gérard Majax and his magic tricks. I learn as he takes a card in his left hand, bends it, checks his mark, and makes it disappear within the deck to find it again. A slick trick. I watch him put a coin behind a spectator's ear and light a candle without a match. Abracadabra, my name is Ahmed, Brio, Steve, and Yasmina. Later we go to the Maurepas garden. We always go with her. Dust from the ground on my feet inside my sandals is annoying in this garden. It comes from the fine dirt, the sand boxes, the side paths, and all the running children who create white dust clouds. The noise and joy of these French children rushing in the public garden of Maurepas offset the pace of my stroll with my great-grandmother, my sister, and the little dog on the leash. It's the law. The sign says: "Dogs on leash only." The light is white in the Maurepas public garden, always. It will remain as such in my memory—white like a nonexistent place, or an invented place, the place of my absence. I don't know who I am any more in the Maurepas garden. A girl? A boy? Marie's great-granddaughter? Rabiâ's granddaughter? Méré's child? Rachid's son? Who? The French girl? The Algerian girl? The Franco-Algerian? On which side of the fence do I stand?

I remain a foreigner. I don't know anyone here who runs, screams, kisses, and seduces, no one. But I see them all and remember them for a long time. I don't know any of these white-skinned people in the white light. The light is white like my great-grandmother's beautiful hair and the bones that uphold her; white like my silenced voice, the color of dead bodies and the hand that holds me. I am embarrassed to be here, overwhelmed by my discomfort. Who am I?

For a long time this sentence will repeat itself when I observe others and fantasize about them. It will betray the ambiguity of my hands and my desiring mouth. Who am I? Thus I go through the garden with its voices and faces that I neither know nor recognize; their names — Marion, Olivier, and Rémi — so different from my name, so easy to pronounce. Is anyone named Yasmina here? Anyone? I walk closely to my great-grandmother, Marie. Marie and her long legs, Marie and her tight belly, Marie and her gnarled hands, Marie is still alive but already close to death by my mere presence, my mere age, our mere differences, and the sadness of the Maurepas garden. Marie and her voice that says: "Heel, Jasmine." Heel, my little body against her hip. And we walk silently under the blue sky of Rennes, a vessel making its way through the garden. Then Marie detaches herself and gets ahead of us. She walks at a good pace with her little dog. And our two bodies follow happily.

The Maurepas garden, its flowery alleys, immense trees, carousels, ice-cream and waffles, the heat of the French summer, French children racing each other for fun: all of this is a change of scenery for us. I remain with Jami, always glued like a leech, clutching like an animal, a marmoset. I hug her tightly, as usual. Jami, for a long time you will remember the swings of Maurepas, green under the gigantic portico. Like small open coffins, they actually can be dangerous. We climb two at a time. Fortunately, I am with my sister, who gives the first push, standing, her knees bent. She sends the swing up toward the sky, knowing how to bend her legs and arc her back. We fly, holding onto the bars. I let her be in charge. I aim for the tops of the trees and further up, even. Later on Sophia will choose the same swing in the park in Paris, and Alexandre after her, just like their mother did. That's the way it is; children all play the same way. They have the same desires; that's the beauty of childhood, its apparent simplicity, and its miracle. And I will watch Sophia fly, her smile, her desire to touch the sky, go over the trees, and get dizzy.

Children's motions, their joys, and their tears are universal. We bestow happiness and vengeance, and reproduce ad infinitum. These perennial activities are passed on from mother to daughter, like a relay, a gift, and a mirror. We swing, we laugh, and we fly. All public gardens resemble Maurepas. They turn into chicken coops suddenly, with little children bursting with joy on the swings. Such innocence.

We fly higher and higher. The little dog watches us, shaking. I hear Marie's voice, in bits and pieces: "Be careful, girls, not so high. Sit down, Nina. You are too small; you're going to fall." That's the way we are, Jami and I. We love the sky more than the land. More than this land, this garden in the city, this French city.

And what about Sophia? Will she fly toward her unknown country, toward Algeria? What will she retain from Bachir and Rabiâ? What will she know of her mother and me on the Maurepas swing, reaching out to the tops of the trees and the blue sky of Rennes? Will we tell her about our afternoons with Marie and her little dog Jasmine? Will we tell her all about our childhood? Will we give her the details? And will I tell her when I hug her: Don't take after me, Sophia. Don't be too sensitive. Don't worry about everything. Make the most of life. Play without thinking. Defend yourself against the violence of others. What will she know of her mother, my protector? Her mother, who used to bend her knees and scream: "Go higher and higher." Her mother used to make me laugh and dream. Yes, Jami, higher. And I fly like we flew away from Tipaza, Algiers, Dar el-Beïda, fleeing my childhood before it came to an end. Here is the unfinished story, little Sophia, little niece. Here, through your childhood, my childhood returns like a ghost that resurfaces through your games, your laugh, your joy, the swings of the park in Paris, and your mother, Jami, who says: "Be careful, Sophia is listening; she understands everything." Be careful. Don't mention: massacres-violence-slaughtered-burnt alive in front of her. Our whispers will not be enough. Algeria devours its people despite the silence, despite the will to hide and protect, despite the soft nest we weave around those we love.

≈

To escape Rennes, my birth place, a stuffy city in the summer. Seventy-five kilometers from Saint-Malo is too far from the sea. To fly away. Leave my grandparents' garden to get our bodies examined. To be cold all of a sudden, cold inside this red dress they force me to wear. For once. For the doctor. Once a summer. A little effort, Nina. To please them and be presentable. Look, your sister has the same one. Cold inside my dress, I feel naked. I hate to start the summer this way, going through this rite that always starts like this: two days in Rennes, see the doctor, then leave for Saint-Malo. It happens almost every summer. I celebrate my birthdays there until I reach eighteen, until I am old enough to say no, until I come of age. No. Until I start living my carefree Parisian life. To go to Brittany and breathe French air, the air of the French sea. The sea that moves, withdraws, and stretches far out in the distance. Go catch the sea, Nina, go. It runs faster than I. It is icy, reddens my skin, and stings my thighs, but nevertheless I secretly go into the water, not waiting for the mandatory two hours needed for digestion. I am not afraid to drown; I know how to struggle with the water and the waves. I am Algerian; I am not afraid of the sea. I almost drowned a thousand times in the surf of Club des Pins, in a whirling eddy at Rocher Plat, in the swimming pool at the Zeralda hotel. I know what it's like: stay calm, go with the flow, believe in myself, and choose life over death. That's the way to avoid drowning. It's also a question of choice. "Let's walk there," says my grandmother. "We will walk by your parents' university." On the street she holds my hand. I am proud. We run into clients: "Hello Madame. What pretty little girls." "Yes, they are here on vacation." I hold on tight to her hand and then to Jami's. I am in the middle, as usual. I feel protected from all these voices that return, these students who say: "Radidja la mouquère." My grandmother has such soft skin, velvet cheeks. Her smell comes from rose-scented soap. I listen to her soft voice telling me about the new constructions, the Thabor flowers, my cousins, our nuclear family. My cousins, my friends, this clan, our clan on Minhic Beach. To swim. To play. To laugh. To love one another. I feel different despite always having been accepted by these children who will become adolescents. Despite always having been accepted by my aunts Fanfan and Aunt J., who will leave us too soon as well. Aunt A., so attentive, covers up everything: our lies, our outings, our exhaustion. She comforts and consoles us from blundering words, petty comments from these neighbors who make fun of me one day: "Radidja la mouquère." It all comes back. Everything starts up again. It's endless. But my grandmother's soft voice is always with me. She asks about Algiers.

La Résidence, the Mitidja's mimosas, the Paradou Street promenade, the delicious small ribs from Hydra's market, and the Deglet Nour dates that we call the sun's fingers. My grandmother came to Algiers to see us and visit the Roman ruins of Tipaza, the Bay of Algiers, Sidi-Ferruch. My grandmother made the trip. I no longer remember where she slept in the apartment. All I remember is her soft, perfumed skin and her small, agile dentist's hands. Her quick diagnosis: cavity, wisdom tooth, and abscesses that need draining. Her laugh echoes in the car in Moretti, then in the house in Saint-Malo, her powerful laugh. It's a sign of her joy of having us, a delight always accompanied by our music. She loves being with her girls, hearing Nina's stories from Mont-Saint-Michel to Saint-Malo. Her scary stories are totally invented. Here is the School of Law and Economics. I don't want to look at the stairs and the auditorium that used to be filled with three hundred students, the place where students sullied my mother. The White woman with the Algerian, the French-Muslim's wife, the students' racism, their disease, a shameful disease entrenched in sex. The fear of the other, the other sex, the other skin, and the fear of dangerous foreigners. No one should ever kill his father. One should remain among Whites. Radidja la mouquère. My grandmother does not say anything. It's all over now. The war is over and so are the sixties. That was all nonsense.

Her two granddaughters are close to her now. One looks like a boy but wears a magnificent red print dress, just this once.

≈

The students sing: "Radidja la mouquère." The French woman, the nasty bitch. She's no different from those who associate with Blacks. Such sharp tongues, like knives. There is no doubt these slanderous words are sexual. There is no doubt racism is a disease, a vice, a shameful disease that flourishes sometimes in the silence of the hearth. They whisper and close the windows. They shout during family meals. The hatred of the other means imagining him against one's own body as if possessed, robbed, penetrated. Racism is a fantasy. It means imagining the smell of another person's skin, his body's tension, the strength of his sex. Racism is a disease like leprosy or necrosis. What bothers them is my mother's body against my father's. These two bodies, their flesh together, their relationship, their union, the rubbing, the heat, this love machine.

I am too fragile to hear all these voices that endlessly repeat the same thing, the voices of these students who have aged and become good fathers and respectable women. I will always be too fragile to hear or comprehend what they say. Always, even at thirty-two, I will be too fragile to know the truth, the unbearable truth. I still hear their voices echoing on the street, a heartfelt cry. It's for real. Words slip out in the subway, on the bus, at the Paris law school, and at dinner parties where vipers infiltrate the conversation. These words disappoint me on the spot. They make me flee. Like acid, they gnaw away the face of the speaker. They haunt me. Call the token Arab, get to know her, invite her and say: "Yes, I know one." Then betray her. But it is not important. No, it's nothing—just an old habit, fragments of the big mosaic, little arrows, and small venom. It is as insignificant as the Algerian children's spit in my mother's blond hair when she sits at the wheel of our blue Citroën.

And what about me? What is my disease? What is the doctor on rue d'Antrain looking for as he inspects my naked body with his hands? What's the point of his questions? He searches my undressed body, feeling my belly, looking at my eyes and ears with a small light beam, flattening my tongue with a small wooden swab, not paying attention. They are only children after all. He makes me walk: Lift your shoulders, hold yourself straight, bend your knees, and extend them now. He listens to my heart, my lungs, and my bronchial tubes. The coldness of his hands, then of his instruments: stethoscope, reflex hammer, and x-ray plates. He searches inside of me for an ailment, as I will search for a long time afterward, for an outside cause to all that has gone wrong: Algeria, my lost friends, France—my solitary country—the smell of Tipaza, a scent of salt, sun, and red earth. My real affliction will be that I no longer see Amine and no longer dive from the cliffs of Rocher Plat. My Algerian affliction runs deep. Hold your breath. Don't move any more; the little bird is coming out: front view, side view, head turned to the left, to the right. Last Name. First name. Age. Citizenship. He whispers in my grandmother's ear. Violent fevers, nausea several times a year. Could it be malaria?

No, but I still get fevers with temperatures of 104 that last two or three days and then subside. Make her drink a lot to rehydrate her body. The sea air of Saint-Malo will be good for her. This here is the real sea. It ebbs and flows in its agitated state and is full of iodine. My health record, vaccinations, weight and size, and the terrible accident I suffered after an eye exam. I was saved at the Mustapha hospital in Algiers. Yes, it was a very bad accident. I remember it. This sentence especially: "We are about to lose Nina," a reiterated phrase. Can't you see that I am losing you, Nina, that we no longer love each other as we did before? Can't you see that we are slowly drowning? Our love is fading and cannot be saved.

I am no longer cold. My skin is burning. I am alive.

≈≈≈

La Varde's cliffs border Saint-Malo's beach. The beach spreads from Minhic to Rochebonne. Immense, it stretches out toward the lights of the fortified city that scintillate at night like low stars on the ocean. Red and sometimes yellow, they align, cold and unreal. Plage du Pont is a sand beach, a very French beach filled with French people. Admission is free even to Arabs, unlike the beaches of the colonial era or the French-only bars and restaurants forbidden to dogs and Arabs. No, Plage du Pont is open to all and free. From their raised white shed, the lifeguards watch the large crowd of white and icy-skinned swimmers. Such agitation. Running into the water, getting out, running fast so as not to catch a cold. I am often near the lifeguard shed: «What are you looking for, buddy?» And later: «Can I invite you for a drink tonight at the Rusty Club?» A lifeboat is stored in the shed. Oxygen bottles, life vests—everything is ready in case of an emergency. Bandages and rubbing alcohol—everything prepared for a potential accident. People drown and fall off the cliffs. Plage du Pont, with its people and their pretty names like Marion and Jacques, is a quiet family beach. On this beach, cold and often drenched by the rain and the great tides, bodies are outstretched awaiting the sun and a tan. These aligned and staggered bodies, on their bellies, on their backs, sitting up, lying diagonally, attest to the despair of being white in the summer. These immobile bodies, frozen in their last gestures, could appear dead from afar. Dead and naked like all these bodies discovered after the B village massacre in Algeria. Children's bodies cut in half, women's bodies split lengthwise like a zipper. Headless men's bodies and bodiless heads, their eyes still open, their stares resembling those of blind people who cannot see anything coming in the night. They did not understand the chaos, the speed, or the panic. They did not see anything: the attackers' faces, the ax falling, or the fire of the torches. No, nothing. It was already too late to see and understand. It was too fast, too strong. Life had already departed without the release from death.

≈≈

Could Plage du Pont hold all these bodies, Algerian bodies, dismembered bodies? Who here will think about this ever? Who here will say: Are you all right, Nina? Can you manage? Isn't it too difficult? What do you dream about at night? What images pass through your mind? Are you able to cope? How do you live with these events? How do you deal with it everyday? How do you hold onto your identity? You know all these places and recognize all the faces. You know them well. And what about Amine? Have you heard from him? Any news? Anything at all about his existence, his truth, his body? Why such sadness in your eyes? It comes at night, when someone else turns into a shadow, a threat, an adversary, an attacker. Why do you lock yourself up at home? Why are you scared of jumping out the window in your sleep? Why is life sometimes a wave that you can no longer ride? You are a great swimmer, though, supple and resilient that you are. And what about Amine? What about his voice, his eyes, and his skin? When did you last see each other? When did this deadly silence begin? When did you stop existing for one another? And why were your violence and your withdrawal misunderstood? Why did you let time pass and distance grow between yourself and other people? Is that a way to protect yourself? And how could you already know what was going to happen in Algeria? How could you know from here in Saint-Malo, on Plage du Pont, among these ghostly bodies?

I am so different on this beach, and it shows. In the seventies people like me are quite rare here, in Brittany. I run fast between the bodies sprawled on the sand. I run to meet the sea that pulls away rapidly, deserting me as if I were unworthy of it. Despite my sister's presence, I often feel alone in my quest for the sea, longing for Rocher Plat, looking for the truth, my Algerian truth. Every picture tells the same story. I look embarrassed, but I always smile at the camera, at my grandmother who is aiming, coaxing me: «A little smile, just a little one.» It's summer; the air is light, the sea is cold, but the sky is so blue. So I smile, standing in front of the hydrangeas outside La Varde's church, in front of Saint-Malo's fortifications, on the deck of the boat that is taking us to Dinard, and on a hydroplane heading to Jersey. I always cling to Jami, who holds me by the shoulders, ensuring her protection and my fragility.

≈≈

I don't know if I am at home here in France. I will never know it, in fact: not in Rennes, not in Saint-Malo, not in Paris. I don't know if I am at home in Algeria either. I will never find out, never confirm this belief, this declaration. I have always felt like an illegal alien going through immigration, like an outlaw always expecting to be picked out from the group of passengers, held by two police officers, surrounded, then dragged to a small room. Who are you? Where do you come from? Where are you going? I have always felt like I am keeping a secret, living a double life, sheltering another self underneath the visible surface. I have always felt like I wear different masks depending on the country, the police officer, and the people I meet.

Where do you come from to be so tanned? From Algiers. I knew it. You could not get that dark here, with those eyes and that skin. There are not too many girls who look like you at the M Club, not many foreigners. But you are pretty in any case.

≈

Don't play beautiful, Nina; I have seen so many profiles like yours in Cairo. You Arabs all look alike: same eyes, same nose, same mouth. Here, it makes waves, but in Cairo or in Marrakech, it's normal. Your features are everywhere on the streets; they are the country's type. I can't even tell that your mother is French. You're like those girls who don't wear the veil. You have the face of the natives, the indigenous and local people. It's an invariable trait, like a flag, a birthmark, or a body type. Over there, I ran into you at least a thousand times.

≈

This morning, on my way back home, standing on top of the fortifications, I threw my swastika pin in the water at high tide. It's gone now, disappeared under the waves. I also want to disappear when I look at you and hear your voice. I so much want to be your friend, Nina. But I know that you don't like me and that you call me the little fascist who lives on rue Blanche.

≈

My friends and I have been looking at you for a long time. Can we ask you a question? Are you Israeli?

≈

How is it at Algiers? Is it really no longer French? What language do you speak over there? Do you go to the French high school? You're not Arab, then? Do you have a photo of your father? What's his name?

≈≈

Maryvonne's daughters are rather small; they are the smallest in the family. It might be from the food or the heat. The sun strikes like an illness over there.

≈≈

To get away from Minhic Beach, to get away from the screaming children in the water and the beckoning voices of their mothers; to get away from the sound of vengeful waves slamming the sand. I find refuge in the isolation and silence of the land, in Rothéneuf, a small village in the countryside, two kilometers away from our vacation house. It's different here, with corn fields, stone houses, a church, and a dog in the garden. Unlike the agitation of the sea, it's tranquil. It evokes a French painting, and it smells like France. It is no longer Algeria. There is no connection, no resemblance. It is the opposite of Algeria: my second country, my double life, the place of assimilation. Here, I must be French, belong, feel good, make friends, and meet people my own age. It is important. Friendship means happiness, my grandmother says. Marion lives in a remodeled mill on the way to Rothéneuf. She has blond hair and blue eyes. She soon becomes my French friend. She has never been to Algeria. She does not know any Algerians and does not speak Arabic—not even a few words like hachma, brel, zarma, kifèche. Nothing. She knows sub-Saharan Africa, having spent her childhood in N'Djamena, but she doesn't know Algeria. She often speaks about Africa, recounting her memories. I say nothing about Algeria, Cherchell, Tipaza, Rocher Plat, my Algerian life, my family, and my friends. Nothing. I am in Rothéneuf. I am assimilated and gravely disloyal. Marion's face slowly replaces Amine's. She enters my existence. She becomes indispensable.

≈≈

I dream about Chad in Saint-Malo. I dream of her Africa, deep and mysterious. Africa, the real thing. Algeria is too close to France, overrun and tethered. I dream of Marion more and more. I envy her. She is the real African girl with blond hair and blue eyes. She is the true foreigner, as my mother has often been herself with her memories and regretful voice. I do not dwell in regrets. I adjust to everything quickly. My ability to adjust is maddening, creating several parallel lives and a multitude of small betrayals.

≈≈

You say that you will love me forever, and I don't believe you. One does not love forever. Things don't happen like that. It's impossible, and you know it, Nina. You live in Algiers, so far from here. You have Algeria, while my world is limited to this beach, Saint-Malo, and the dike at night. I walk there, under La Varde's cliffs, looking really far beyond the sea, praying that you will hear me, feel me, see me. It's a call from your land to mine, from my boredom to your life force. Always waiting, waiting for summer and your return. Some day you will no longer return to Saint-Malo, and you will erase everything, as you erase everything so fast. You will no longer want to or be able to. It will become too difficult, too personal. Locked up in your Algerian misery, you will no longer keep in touch.

≈≈

My grandmother seems so happy in Saint-Malo. She gets reborn, she says. It's from the ocean air and the surf hitting her body. I hear her sudden laugh in the small vacation house. Winding through the bedrooms, it spreads like a contagion. When I turn up the music, she often sings and dances: "Oh, I want to hold you so much. I love you, baby. I can't take my eyes off you."[25] When our other cousins, Jami, and I are here together, she says it's a party. A real gang, we are all from the same family. But these two granddaughters come from so far away. It is different with them; it's a special

25. These lyrics are in English in the original text. —*Translators*

relationship that implies more responsibility. What if something happened? How would she tell Rachid about his two daughters, his two marvels? This is real love, a newfound love, a revived story. She says that she will miss the joy, the music, the lack of self-consciousness, and the freedom. She says childhood heals everything, and these summer months spent together are a real pleasure. Later she won't understand my absence, my silence, or my adult life, secret and closed.

≈≈

Every morning I scrutinize myself. I have four problems. Am I French or Algerian? Am I a girl or a boy?

≈≈

We buy crabs. The poor little things are still alive; we have to throw them in boiling water and put the lid on top. It is cruel. Everyone is screaming in the small vacation house. We close our eyes to this brutality, since we love crab so much. We just have to close our eyes, ignore these boiled creatures and their claws scraping the sides of the pot. Ignore them, just like we will ignore the children from M's village burnt alive. Ignore these human cinders, their surprised gazes and outstretched hands beckoning us.

≈≈

At night I escape from the small vacation house through my bedroom window. I just need to jump and run really fast. I go down to the beach and look at the sea. I guess where it is from the sound of the slow, flowing waves at high tide. I look at the horizon toward the beam of the lighthouse, this vital sign. At night the dark beach resembles a forest. I think about Amine so much: his voice, his hands, his skin, his shoulders, and his body slowly becoming that of a man. I think about him so as not to forget him. It's the price I have to pay, my punishment. I imagine him hearing my voice carried by the ocean and feeling my presence. I know he forgets me too. Summer is a cruel and extreme season. In the hellish summer, the sun and the sea join with a soft wind that perfumes my hair. Summer divides. Summer exposes everything. Summer disrupts equilibrium. It is because of the sky, its deep blue color. It is because of vertigo and frenzy.

≈≈≈

Amine and Nina: the most uttered words—a beloved incantation that becomes the cruelest.

≈≈≈

A sudden absence. These words that used to be on everyone's lips. But then, suddenly: Nina, just Nina. The word *Amine* is now missing from the calling of my name, obliterated from the French language. Amine is absent from my fantasy world, my life.

≈≈≈

With his absence, I lose my other name, my mirror. I will not say anything about Amine or our separation to anyone. No, nothing. I will not talk about this loss, neither in Algiers nor in Saint-Malo. I will say nothing of his mother's injunction: "I do not want my son to keep seeing her." I will not talk about my bad influence on him to anyone. I will not talk about my love.

≈≈≈

We all search for Amine. Our whole life long. Tensed. We all seek paradise in another face, in other eyes. The enchantment of recognizing oneself in another, marveling at oneself, finding one's other half. Amine is the longing for connection, innocence, and happiness. Algeria. Amine is the missing piece. Amine is the sadness that marks the end of summer. In my real life, Amine is the given name.

≈≈≈

Where are you, Amine?

≈≈≈

Here, I forget Algeria, its men, its warmth, and the color of the sea. It's a betrayal. I forget the violence and the fear. I forget the need to constantly look over my shoulder to verify that nothing is there, though my intuition tells me that something could happen. Here, I embrace my French side, becoming a subject not yet fully formed, living a lie. Who am I truly? I adopt a Parisian accent, speaking French, my mother tongue. I speak in French only. I dream in French only. I will write in French only. Arabic is a sound, a song, and a voice that I retain and feel but don't master. Arabic is an emotion, expressed in the voices of Faïrouz and Abdel Wahab. It's another self that I shelter, a small wound. Algeria does not flourish on my tongue; it takes root in my body. Algeria does not shape my words. Algeria surfaces in what devours me. Algeria is in my body; it emerges when I am out of control, excessive, demanding, and strong-willed. Algeria is in my mad desire to be loved.

≈≈

My grandmother loves me more and more. She shows tenderness in her hands that caress my face and wash my body, in her voice that never yells at me or at Jami, and in her softness and caring attention. She is delighted to see us here on French soil.

≈≈

At high tide we all go down to the beach after dinner, all of us: my grandmother, our cousins, friends, the seasonal residents, and the little dog. The ocean is powerful, says my grandmother, with its foaming rolls and tentacle-like currents that come and snatch away incautious swimmers—their prey. The sea reaches the lifeguard shed. It hits the levee. At high tide, when the sea is less agitated, I dive. I have to be swift. It's a pleasurable swim in the warm and calm water following all that turbulence. Then I go back up the stone stairs, a bit shaken, but I don't say anything. My grandmother wraps me in a terry cloth towel, rubbing with all her strength, erasing the memory of the retreating sea, the currents, and the night falling on the washed-out beach. But I run away from her arms; I start all over again, diving in the great waves of the equinox tide. I disobey. I am not afraid any more. I am loved.

≈≈≈

I get used to French life, its quietness, my getting to know Marion, her face, her blue eyes, her voice, and her promises.

≈≈≈

I take the little dog in my arms, protecting him from the wind and the noise of the waves. I feel his heart beating underneath my hand. My grandmother is right. The heart of a little dog is fragile. It contains all of our solitude.

≈≈≈

Swimming at high tide, going around the levee, being a child on the deck of the boat that takes us to Dinard, being a teenager, jumping on a moped, hitchhiking to town, drinking a terribly bitter cup of coffee, always rebuffing those who want to kiss me, dancing and singing, and going to the Rusty Club and the Penelope Club: so this is what vacation is like for a young French woman.

≈≈≈

Here, I don't talk about Algeria to anyone. Why not? I don't say anything about Amine, his face, or who he is. I don't ever say anything about the city, the sea, or the desert. Why not? I don't say anything about the rising violence that smothers us and shrinks our territory or about how we must beware of isolated places, avoiding deserted beaches, the remote countryside, and roads after 6:00 p.m. I don't talk about my attempted kidnapping, the exact details of the man's face, the trauma of this true story, this early lesson. Why not? I don't have any photos with me, no evidence. I bring nothing from Algeria, its people, or my life over there. I lie by omission.

≈≈≈

It is not because of shame, no, certainly not. I am not ashamed of also being Algerian. I never was, as a matter of fact. I am proud of it and use it to be provocative and arrogant. At times I will squelch my French side in order to avenge my childhood silences, my omissions. It is not because of fear either. I am not afraid of the words *wog, sand nigger, rat*. I can hear them, letting them wash over me, drown me. They always give me strength—the strength that comes from hatred, the strength to fight, and be myself. No, it is not that. Discomfort is what it's all about. The problem is that I'm not talking about the same subject, the same land, the same sea, the same beach, or the same friends any more. I become a stranger to the other person, and the other person becomes a stranger to me because Algeria sets me apart instantly and creates two opposing sides. Because of its past and its present. That's the problem. It's in the distance, the rifts, and the altered relationships. It's in the building of walls, the digging of ditches, and the slamming of doors. It's in the erasure of my talent, my terrible ability to adapt: my complete negation.

≈≈

And who could understand my longing to feel, brush, and hold Amine, Algiers, La Résidence? Who could hear our beckoning voices under the wisteria, between the orange trees, and near the olive grove? Who could become one with nature's warm and endearing sensuality? And who will remember me here? Who will say some day: It is horrible, awful, and unbearable? And who will write to me: Dear Nina, wherever you are, I think about you. I know that you are strong, but still, how can you stand it all? The violence, the events, the Algerian situation?

≈≈

And in turn I will repeat every day. But how do my Algerian friends do it? How do they manage to live their lives, fall asleep at night, and dream?

≈≈

Silenced by my secret, I don't say anything when I'm in Saint-Malo. Who forced me anyhow to remain quiet and keep to myself? Who forced me to internalize everything from the very beginning? My silence is a body. My silence is a house. My silence is a habit. My silence is a fortress. I must not say anything; I have to just stare ahead and hold back my tears. I must hear without responding. I must not tell, but where will I get the strength to speak, to write? How will I write without regrets? How will I write without being afraid of other people's judgments, their questions? How will I not fear my own answers? How do I keep track of all these unessential facts? How do I communicate all of it: everything I write, everything I repeat like the babble of a rude child or the words of a lying child?

≈≈

Here, French families meet every summer. The beach becomes a meeting place where we find last season's faces again. With a heavy heart, we search for them among all the bodies, their nakedness. Running toward friends, we greet each other. The beach is a place of remembrance, unlike Moretti, Sidi-Ferruch, Tipaza—these places, mostly deserts, with dramatic coastlines, cliffs, and reefs. Algerian beaches are brutal, magnificent and brutal. The encounter with nature—its smell, its strength, and the sensation of transcendence—is immediate. Algerian beaches do not invite reunions; acquaintances and families don't meet there. People avoid facing themselves. The sea, the sun, and the cliffs are the sole companions to all the unmoored bodies. Later it is difficult to feel integrated, to acknowledge people, to greet them, and to become a part of my French family.

≈≈

In the evening the beach belongs to the town residents. Pounded by the swimmers, burnt by the sun, it looks different and scarred. Sometimes we decide to walk to Saint-Malo along the beach. Following the slope toward Davier and Sézambre islands, I go with my aunts F., J., A., and my cousins. I finally break into this clique;

we hold hands like a true gang. I feel different, but I feel good and strong; it is exciting to explore and advance in unknown French territory: Le Pont, Le Minhic, Paramé, Rochebonne, and Saint-Malo.

≈≈

In Algeria I can stay above the water for a long time balancing on a rock, sometimes for a whole hour. I'm not sensitive to the sun, and time is on my side. There, I learn about patience and contemplation. There, I learn to write, laying the foundation for my future life.

≈≈

Nobody calls me Yasmina in Saint-Malo. It is a voluntary erasure. I always initiate it, introducing myself with this little sting: Nina.

≈≈

I refuse to show my passport photo, hiding my true identity.

≈≈

Amine, you call me Yasmina but not in front of other people. It is your secret, your way of being a man. You say "Yesmina," the Algerian way, emphasizing the Y. It gives you strength, the authority of a man over a woman. It signifies your domination over me and your desire. When uttered by you, "Yesmina" becomes more feminine. It's a fleeting game, a role that we abandon easily as we dive from the cliffs of Rocher Plat like two angels.

≈≈

When I think of France, I hear the cooing of the doves in the garden of the vacation house, their song, and the smell of the bakery, warm bread and croissants. I see France in the colors of the candy bins, Chupa Chups, Malabar, Carambar, white flour, and salted butter. For me, France is the taste of pleasure.

≈≈

They have family houses, family furniture, family paintings, big parks, and gravel alleys. They eat family meals. They tell family stories. They have their place in their family tree. Smothered.

≋

I feel very free in Algeria. There are always four of us, four against everyone else. We are only four in the Bouraoui family, four against the world's adversity. Four against them, the four of us withdraw. Four is a lucky number: four card players, four little-horse players, four Mille Bornes players; the number four creates a perfect square like the four sharp corners of our home.

≋

There are so many of us in Saint-Malo. We set up big tables for ten to fifteen cousins, their parents, and our grandfather. He drives from Rennes on Sundays with his mother, Marie, in his American car. All these voices, laughs, and opinions mixed together are overwhelming. So are the whispers, the buzzing secrets, and the festive meal. I am often cold. My hair wet from the last swim, I shiver violently despite the sun's rays on the garden, the table, and my body. But it's not a sign of fever; it's a feeling of panic overwhelming my senses like a snake slithering under my skin. I am shaken by my self-consciousness when I am in social situations. It's from being surrounded by too many people. Exceeding the number four, I feel alone and naked. There are only two of us here. Jami and I are detached from the rest of the family in spite of ourselves, by the mere story of our secluded life in Algeria—a life that impedes mingling and sharing. Rachid and Maryvonne's daughters: two girls alone. In spite of the laughs, the apparent happiness, and my grandmother's hands on my shoulders, I am cold in Saint-Malo: You are frozen, Nina. I told you not to swim so early. You're not in Algeria here. You're not used to this cold water. But it is neither the sea nor the wind that makes me cold; it is my loneliness. It's the discomfort of looking at them all so carefully and the feeling of robbing them, studying each face, recalling their voices and their words, taking something from them. It is my discomfort at watching this family scene, my family that reunites in the quiet, French summer.

≈≈

We are allowed to climb into the Buick, turn the steering wheel, push on the pedals, and beep the horn—but no more than three times. Our grandfather lets us look in the rearview mirror, fasten the seat belts, and drive the unmoving car.

≈≈

Marie does not go down to the beach. She remains in the garden in a lounge chair, hiding from the sun though it is very faint. She stays in the thicket of trees, her hands clasped, remaining still. She often says she's waiting for death to come.

≈≈

I sit near her. I don't like this beach on Sundays either. It's too noisy and busy with all the running, screaming children who throw sand at each other. And I don't like my body on this beach. I remain in the garden, talking to Marie, but she does not answer. She keeps her eyes closed, pretending to be sleeping.

≈≈

Sunday afternoons fly by. They start at three p.m. after a long lunch. Everyone is busy trimming the hedge, fixing the gravel, or getting the sailboard ready. We play in the dune, a sloped area along the side of the house. We fold the garden table. We rest. I wake up Marie by unclasping her hands. I am so scared of death.

≈≈

My grandfather goes down to the beach. He remains at the top of the stone stairs. Surveying everything from Minhic to Saint-Malo, he stares. He inspects everything like a landowner would, exuding the kind of happiness that comes from the sea, its sound, color, waves, and smell.

≈≈

Voices are lowered. Someone whispers in my grandmother's ear. Family secrets told behind closed doors. Fingers pressed against their lips. Whispers. Fleeting eyes. I am not in on the secret, but I guess what it is.

≈≈

During this summer in France, I hide Ahmed deep down. I don't answer to voices that say: "buddy," "young man," "sir-ma'am." "Is that your grandson?" When this happens, I don't look at my grandmother. I know she does not like my ambiguity, but my clothes, my gait, my haircut are not the root of the problem. All children look alike and blend in. The problem lies in the desire to hide, dissimulate, and transform oneself. The problem lies in the desire to escape from the self like an outlaw, disconnected from one's being.

≈≈

They return to Rennes — by train or by car — in the bright and pink sky of the summer evening. The men of my family often work regardless of vacation time. My aunts stay behind with their sons and daughters, while I stay behind with Jami. Marie waves her hand behind the window of the American car that takes her toward the city. She's heading for the small Maurepas apartment filled with memorabilia from the ocean liner captain: black statues, frozen stiff. Her mirrors.

≈≈

All Sunday evenings are alike, even during vacation at the shore. Sundays are out of the ordinary: life, movement, the promise of eternal love, the anticipation of seeing each other again. All Sunday evenings are sad: low tide evenings, when everything gets motionless and dissolves, nostalgic evenings, when everyone here seems to regret something or carry a secret inside.

≈

And what is the secret of this woman who walks along the water on Minhic Beach? This woman with her back turned to me, my grandmother, whom I look at against her will. She walks barefoot in the sand carrying her shoes. She walks alone, in the pink, yellow, and red sunset that will soon get mixed in the blue of the sea. The last rays, green and slowly disappearing. What is she thinking about here on this beach? What is she dreaming of in her solitude? Where is the true life of this woman who loved the piano so much and who still loves to sing and dance? Does she love me? What is the secret behind her face, so sad at times? What is the secret behind her silences and absences? This woman appears to flee, walking closely to the sea, as if she were trying to get strength from its immensity, as if it were her time to go far away, leaving her life behind. Is she happy walking close to the waves of this cold and frozen sea that transports her? This woman sometimes looks at me without seeing me truly, hears me without knowing me, and walks without feeling my gaze following her. This woman no longer wants to stop walking. What is her connection to my mother? What remains and gets passed on? This woman does not know that I watch her from the lifeguard shed and that I protect her, in my own way.

TIVOLI

It took place in Tivoli during that incredible summer. I did not go to Saint-Malo that year but went to Rome instead. It was a scorching summer, unlike any other. It took place in the Tivoli gardens during this auspicious season—the season of visible bodies. It took place amidst the humid trees, drenched alleys, and flowing waterfalls, where the young men, the *ragazzi*, played in the water, their torsos bared. They laughed and shouted and seemed so happy to be there. Their bodies, full of desire, glistened in the sun and in the water. She and I stayed at the Grand Hôtel, in a good-sized double room including a white bathroom with tub, a small balcony, and interior shutters—such a beautiful room. The hotel stood atop the Piazza di Spagna, blazing with crimson flowers.

It was warmer than in Algiers. The sea, its waves and breezes, had been replaced with Rome's scorching stones. But I was used to the heat, its assault, and asphyxiation. I knew how to live with it. I often dressed in white to protect myself from the light and to prepare for what was about to happen to me. We walked a lot in Rome. We forgot Algiers, its climate, and its insecurity. We sought greater freedom everywhere we went: at night, in deserted streets, in remote areas, and in the Tivoli gardens. Everything was so easy there: being oneself, taking a walk, staying out late, and looking around. Walking among these men and women, I was no longer afraid of anything. I was no longer French. I was no longer Algerian. I was not even my mother's daughter anymore. I was myself, comfortable with my body, in the Coliseum, the Forum, via Venetto, del Corso, del Popolo, and Trevi. I had the feeling that something was about to happen. In all the churches, I rediscovered darkness and silence. Because the heat is a cry, a roar. Combined with light, it's a tear.

We tried to stay cool by any means necessary. We ate shaved frozen coconut, gelati, and fruits, especially oranges, and went to the Tivoli gardens.

During that exceptional Roman summer, I wanted to see everything, visit everything, and know about everything, as if I were never going to return. Temples, ruins, palaces, a living history—Rome is my city, my new city with its men and women, such exhilarating beauty.

Looking at the blue sky there, I never felt like crying.

I became happy in Rome. I tied my hair back. We discovered a thin nape. Sensitive ties. A pretty face. Eyes that turned green in the sun. Female hands and gestures. A deeper and controlled voice. I became happy in Rome. My body revealed something new, an evidence, a different personality, a gift, perhaps. I came from myself and myself alone. I was finding myself, born solely from my eyes, my voice, and my desires. I shed my old self and reclaimed my identity. My body was breaking free. It no longer had French traits. It no longer had Algerian traits. It experienced the simple joy of being alive, a joy so powerful that it can be seen in all the photographs from this trip: at the Grand Hôtel entrance, on the steps of the Piazza di Spagna, in the back of a red horse carriage, in the Forum, and in the midst of the Roman ruins. But it was no longer Tipaza, and it was not Chenoua either. Everything was changing--my skin, my vision. Nothing would ever be the same again in my lone body. My aura changed. My body had decided to be free in the Tivoli gardens, free with the *ragazzi* dancing around me as I remained immobile in front of the camera lens. Like an eye, it focused on me as the center of everything, integrating me into a simple life. Like a witness, it captured the shoulders, the belly, the naked backs of the boys of summer, their screams, their joy, their beauty, and the noise of the huge waterfall wetting my hair, just for the photo.

They spoke to me. Without understanding their language, I became aware of my own power through their words, their songs, and a new force haunting my body: my desire.

AMINE

Dear Amine,

When I returned from Rome, you had changed. You looked at me differently. Your eyes, your hands, and your lips were no longer the same. You hesitated before opening the door. You didn't recognize me. I had stopped by without calling. I wasn't sure I would find you. You let me in, but you didn't want to. I could tell. I remember it very well. Your mother found me beautiful, repeating many times: "Your hair looks nice like that, Nina." She seemed happy. But you said nothing about me. Nothing. I was dressed in white. My body had changed during this odd Roman summer. It had experienced desire. And you sensed it, Amine. I saw it when you glanced at my belly and mouth, averting your eyes as if you had been singed. You were angry with me, perhaps feeling betrayed, yet I was there, in front of you, with you. You were already withdrawing into your silence, initiating our separation, and guarding the secret that would mark the end of our shared life. It was late August, early September. In Algeria the fragrance of orange trees was still strong, as was that of jasmine and wisteria. For the first time we didn't go to your room. Instead, we remained among the other people, for protection. We listened to their voices that echoed in the living room. We drank iced tea. It was very hot. You still covered your mouth with your hand, and you lowered your eyes when I tried to make eye contact. We both talked about our vacations: Rome, the stones, the ruins, the relics. I had the feeling I was telling the end of our story. We said goodbye. We kissed each other rather firmly, for the first time ever, like a man and a woman, and you didn't walk me to the door.

We often crossed paths afterward. Without speaking or looking at each other, we knowingly avoided one another like blind people who sense an obstacle nearby. Without knowing it, you sometimes inspired me to write. Remembering you, so fully and constantly, I wrote stories to fill the emptiness and the void you left inside of me despite yourself. I wrote to compensate for my longing and to fill the holes in my story. Your story probably has them as well. The emptiness gnaws at us. There will always be a trace of you on my skin, Amine. It's a small blue tattoo, the color of the sky of Algiers. Something of us will always remain, Amine, in our dreams, in our strength, and in this joy of rediscovering the scent of Algeria that, by some miracle, returns every year in France with the arrival of spring.

To order or obtain more information on these or other University of Nebraska Press titles, visit www.nebraskapress.unl.edu.

Lightning Source UK Ltd.
Milton Keynes UK
UKOW05f0609241116
288424UK00017B/67/P